CAT AND MOUSE MURDER

When Chris receives a phone call from Ruth frantically asking for his help, he assumes it is a ruse to stop him ending their affair. Feeling obliged to go to her, he finds Ruth in a state of terror — scratched, bruised and frightened to go home. Soon an unpleasant and bizarre sequence of events is unfolding, and the escalating game of cat and mouse leaves a young woman lying dead in a grimy city alley. Lieutenant Joe Dickerson will need all of his cunning and ingenuity to uncover the killer . . .

EATON K. GOLDTHWAITE

CAT AND MOUSE MURDER

Complete and Unabridged

LINFORD
Leicester

First published in Great Britain

First Linford Edition
published 2020

A catalogue record for this book is available
from the British Library.

ISBN 978–1–4448–4447–4

Published by
Ulverscroft Limited
Anstey, Leicestershire

Set by Words & Graphics Ltd.
Anstey, Leicestershire
Printed and bound in Great Britain by
T. J. International Ltd., Padstow, Cornwall

This book is printed on acid-free paper

For MARIE who has been very patient and very kind

1

Aware that she had not been reading for some time, the girl closed her book and thrust it aside. Rising, she stretched, and lifting herself on bare toes moved to the wide window, pulled back the drape and looked down.

The street was barren, windswept and glistening with patches of rain. Premature leaves from discouraged plane trees performed a tired, fitful ballet; a shower of raindrops, like quick-starting tears, blurred street lamps and neon signs and other windows behind which other people watched or waited or did not care.

This street: she had loved it once, had worshipped and adored all that it represented. Adventure, romance, opportunity, freedom, recognition; it had not seemed drab or dingy or barren then.

Her eyes closed and her hand tightened on her throat. It has been two weeks now, she thought. Two weeks consisting of

fourteen days: fourteen mornings, noons, afternoons and nights. You did not mind the days. You could lose yourself in yards of fabrics and papers, surround yourself with mahogany, blond maple, satinwood, bronzes, mirrors; form and colour depth, perspective, effect.

But the nights —

Sighing, she opened her eyes and turned to stare unseeing at the room. Once she had loved this room, had put into it all the cumulative results of taste and training, and most of her savings. The Duncan Phyfe drop-leaf table, rescued from ignominious obscurity in a junk shop; without seeing she knew every brass mount on the curule-shaped legs, every carving of the plinth over which her hands had so lovingly and anxiously worked. The Winthrop desk, the Chippendale chair, framed faience tiles, girandole mirror — material things, but she had loved them.

That did not give them the right to oppress her now.

I am a fool, she thought.

Shaking her head she moved to the

desk, opened it and seating herself found blue notepaper and a pen and began to write. She wrote swiftly, surely, in a clear and beautiful script:

Dear Bill — I was deeply shocked to read in the newspapers concerning your domestic difficulties. I almost telephoned you, and then I thought that since Marge and I had been friends —

No.
Frowning, she tore the sheet in half, selected another and began anew:

Dear Bill — I have been working a bit too hard and thought that your agency might find me a cottage in Chelmere; any sort of place, furnished, where I could spend weekends until winter sets in —

She had finished, addressed and sealed it and was staring at nothing when the door buzzer sounded. She turned, startled, and a flush coloured her cheeks.

Quickly she dashed, found her shoes and put them on. 'Coming!' she called and sped to the mirror, pushed at her hair, smoothed her dress, and ran, then walked, to the foyer.

A man, undistinguished, neither young nor old. He was wearing overalls and a sweater and his face was turned shyly downward. 'Thought you might like to see the final edition, Miss Cassell.' His voice was thin, embarrassed.

'Oh — oh, thank you, George. That's very thoughtful of you.'

She accepted the newspaper. Closing the door she turned and leaned against it. Slowly the newspaper dropped down; the colour receded from her cheeks and her shoulders sagged wearily.

I *am* a fool, she thought.

★   ★   ★

Christopher Elliot crossed the wide entrance hall, shedding outer garments as he walked. Retrieving the evening newspaper from a pocket he hung both topcoat and hat in the hall closet, moved to the foot of the curving stair and called up, 'Hello! I'm home!'

'Hello, Chris.' From the upper recesses Henrietta's voice floated down. 'Dinner in about fifteen minutes — we're having lamb. Will you make a cocktail?' The last of her response was both strengthened by the opening of a door and obscured by the clatter of shoes along the upper hall.

Young Wickie, breathless as usual, came pounding down the stairs.

'Hello, Daddy. Gee, you're home early. Got the paper? Daddy, will you let me have mice? A boy at school has some. He let me pet 'em. Please, Daddy, the *paper* — Mommy's going to read us the funnies — '

Christopher listened with only the upper tenth of his brain. Happily he caught his small son from the stairs and briefly scuffled with him, and then quickly gave up in pretence of being mortally wounded. It was a game of which they never tired.

Wickie, newspaper in hand, escaped to clamber in breathless triumph up the stairs while Christopher, chuckling, retraced his steps halfway along the hall to enter his study.

Once inside, with the door carefully closed, the smile faded from Christopher's eyes. He walked, a little tiredly, to his desk and switched on the fluorescent light there.

From his side pocket he withdrew a blue envelope. Tentatively he lifted it and sniffed at the faintest of elusive scents, then grimacing, pulled out a folded note sheet.

On it was written, simply and in elegant script, *Will telephone you tonight at nine.*

There was no signature, nor did there need to be. He had found it on the seat of his car, and that too posed no special question; she might be visiting someone in Chelmere, or possibly she had a house to do. He had no way of telling how long the note had been there, for the car had been standing in the station plaza since morning.

The only problem was that she was here in Chelmere and would call him; it was not like her to do a thing of this sort.

But then he could scarcely blame her. His recent aloofness must be as baffling to her as his previous attention had so abruptly come to be inexplicable to himself.

He was not quite sure what he should do.

He hesitated, annoyed by his indecision, and then he heard footsteps descending the stairs. From the calm and measured tread he knew it was Henrietta. She would be coming down for last-minute instructions to Agnes; this duty dispatched she would appear to claim her cocktail.

Hurriedly Christopher left the desk and strode to the fireplace. Taking his lighter from his waistcoat pocket he lit the wick and held the tiny flame to the corner of the blue envelope. He watched stolidly as the flame curled upward; the envelope burned more rapidly than did the enclosure and the process required dexterous handling to avoid singeing his fingers.

He held on until only a small corner remained and then he dropped the burning ash.

On the mantel was a square clock that was very old; it had been a wedding gift from Henrietta's brother Warwick. Below the face of the clock was a mirror, framed by gilt pillars, and upon it some long-dead doltish craftsman had engraved:

It is later than you think.

Christopher, as he turned away, caught the reflection of a face that somehow did not belong to him, for the ordinarily ruddy cheeks were grey and the usually exuberant blue eyes were introspective and tired.

* * *

Christopher was feeling cross and out of sorts, but he made a swift attempt to master it. 'What are we in for tonight?' he asked as he put his Old Fashioned on a tile-topped stand and established himself in his favourite chair.

Henrietta paused before a bowl of chrysanthemums and rearranged them deftly. She was a tallish woman, the top of her head reaching nearly to the level of

Christopher's eyes, and her body and limbs were beautifully proportioned. Her grace was tempered with a definite efficiency.

'I thought it might be fun to play some bridge,' she answered. 'We've done so little entertaining lately.' Her voice was low and throaty; it went with the quick colour that mounted to her fine dark eyes.

'Bridge?' His heart sank.

'I've asked the Brokaws and Lyman Ashton.' Bringing her drink she came to sit on the divan opposite him. 'And I thought perhaps Cissie Folwell — I know you dislike her, but she does play very well.'

'Doesn't she, though. The trick is in getting her to shut up long enough to play.' He exhaled in vexation. Bridge! A house full of people on this night, of all nights. 'I suppose that means we'll have Wick and Elaine also.'

The unconcealed bitterness in his voice made her hesitate momentarily. 'Yes, Wick and Elaine.' She paused and her colour deepened. 'Chris, I wish you'd — '

'You wish that I'd be nice to Wick? Of

course. In spite of the fact he doesn't seem to approve of me, I invariably try. At least I try to remember that he's your brother. You'd think that after being a member of the family nearly nine years I might be accepted, even by Wick. Even if he does happen to be Warwick Geer the Second, Rhodes scholar, curator of the Folwell Museum, pillar of the church — '

'Stop it!' Her face was flushed and angry little lights flecked her eyes. 'You needn't be sarcastic; perhaps I am even more aware than you of his faults. I realize how spoiled he is, how conceited and egotistical, but there is much more to him than that. If only you wouldn't try to patronize him.' Her glance wavered and suddenly her voice broke. 'Oh, Chris, please! I don't want to argue. I make some concessions too. You know I can't stand Arthur Brokaw and the horrible creatures he is always getting himself married to, but I put up with him and with them for your sake.' Her hand came up to her forehead. 'Oh, Chris, why are we always arguing? What's come over us? What's happening to us?'

A new fear added to the turmoil in Christopher's mind; his glance sharpened and instantly he became wary, defensive. 'Us?' he repeated. 'Why, there's nothing wrong, is there?'

She neither answered nor met his eyes.

'It's my fault, and I'm sorry,' he said slowly. 'I didn't mean to go off like that. I really like Wick. To tell the truth, I suppose I resent him because he's always made me feel I don't deserve you, and I'm afraid he's right. But I'll try. I honestly will try.'

Her head came up and he saw that tears were in her eyes. He was surprised, for she was not a woman given to displays of emotion. She grinned, a bit forlornly. 'Thanks, Chris. I know you will. I — I'm sorry, too, darn it. I was quite unfair to Arthur.'

'I'll meet you halfway on Arthur's 'creatures'. This latest one: his fifth, isn't she? *Lambie Pie.*

'The name fits her so nicely.' Rising, she started a few steps and then stopped by the chrysanthemum bowl. Without turning she asked, 'You — you hadn't planned to go out tonight? You're sure you won't mind having them in?'

'Mind? No. Perhaps it will be fun. Matter of fact, I'm beginning to like the idea.'

She turned and her face was thoughtful. She seemed about to speak; it was apparent that she was preoccupied. But whatever it was she translated into a sigh.

Averting her eyes she asked, 'Would you mind running up to see Teena for a minute? The poor baby was feverish and I put her to bed.'

'Teena sick?' Christopher came quickly to his feet. 'Of course I'll go up. I wish you'd let me know. You might have phoned me. I'd have brought her something from town.'

*   *   *

At precisely nine o'clock when Christopher was summoned to the telephone he made his exit as nonchalantly as he could, but inwardly he was raging. As far as he could see, the situation could scarcely have been worse. Despite her wealth or possibly because of it, Cissie Folwell possessed the most actively vicious tongue in Chelmere. During the less than an hour of alleged bridge, Cissie had dissected the love lives of everyone so unfortunate as to come within her range. The miserable presence of Arthur Brokaw's partner *pro tem* had not spared him from review and his soft pink hide quivered abjectly as each new shaft struck home; fortunately 'Lambie Pie' was either extremely stupid or else extraordinarily forbearing.

It was not as if Arthur Brokaw were a nobody; although he might, as Cissie unkindly proclaimed, look like a Western Union messenger boy gone to seed. Arthur owned either through inheritance or acquisition half the houses in Chelmere; he had outsmarted the Folwell estate in a couple of deals, and that was probably why the money-hungry Cissie would give him no surcease.

And Wick: Warwick Geer was in one of his moods. Missing neither syllable nor opportunity, through deft manoeuvres he kept egging Cissie on, at one and the same time currying her favour — she was his boss — and, out of his hate for her, encouraging her to display her most unlovely characteristics. Poor Arthur! And poor Lyman Ashton. Sheep among wolves. Well, this should give Ashton material for his books —

None too gently, Christopher closed the door on Cissie's latest blast. He followed the patient Agnes to the telephone and there waited for her to complete her journey to the kitchen.

Just by chance he looked up, and on the dark stair above saw a flushed, shining little face.

'Teena! You're supposed to be in bed!'

'The te-phone waked me up, Daddy. I'm thirsty an' my throat hurts. I want a drink of water.'

'Go back to bed. I'll be up in a minute. No — Agnes, will you get Teena a drink and see that she's tucked in?'

He waited while Agnes laboriously climbed the stairs. When he heard a door close and the sound of water being drawn he picked up the telephone, and the greyness returned to his face.

'Chris? This is Ruth. I seem to have interrupted something; did you get my note?'

'Y-yes.' His tongue did not want to behave. 'It was Teena. She's ill. The telephone always — ' He glanced around and then, in a lower tone, answered, ' — yes, I received your note.'

'I'm sorry. I didn't know that your daughter was ill and I really didn't mean to wake her.'

'Oh, it's all right. Naturally you wouldn't have known.' Silly, inane, stupid. What does one say? What was it he had meant to tell her? Something abrupt, formal and final. See here, Ruth, this is no good — that was to be it, but how? Why didn't he just hang up and walk back in there, throw them all out, and then tell Henrietta

'What did you say, Chris? You sound so funny, as if you were far away. I wanted to let you know that I've taken a cottage in Chelmere; we're practically neighbours. I'll be here nights and week-ends — Bill Donath found it for me. On Echo Road; you can't possibly miss it. The first white

15

house beyond the curve after you pass over the bridge. Won't you drop down for a drink? It's quite early. I haven't seen you in a long time, Chris.'

This isn't real, Christopher thought. It's just something I'm dreaming. I'll come out of it; in a minute now I'll reach out across the dark to touch Henrietta's hand.

He said, 'We have guests. I don't see how I could possibly get away.'

'But after they've gone?' The bantering note dropped from her voice. 'I — I want to see you, dear. It — it's been frightful.'

'All right, I'll try,' Christopher sighed.

★ ★ ★

At half-past ten, when Agnes appeared with the refreshments, the last pretences of bridge disappeared. It could not truthfully be said that the party had been an unqualified success. Toward the end the play had bogged down badly and there had been an undercurrent of which Christopher, already distraught, was all too keenly aware. Henrietta had been

16

more than usually reserved; several times, after his return from the telephone, he caught her fine dark eyes in the act of probing and weighing him. When he sought to get nearer to her she withdrew, holding herself close to Elaine Loring, the plain and proper girl whom Wick would someday get around to marrying.

In a huff, Christopher turned his attention to Arthur Brokaw; Arthur was his most important client, and more than that he liked to think of him as a friend. But Cissie's barbs had done their work. Arthur's pink-faced sensitiveness had changed to pale and sullen watchfulness. Monosyllabic at best, Arthur was reduced to unintelligible grunting and he stayed by Lambie Pie, holding firmly on to her hand.

It had affected them all; even the sage and personable Lyman Ashton felt the tension, although he reacted in quite a different way. Older and more experienced than the rest of them, Ashton tried valiantly to pull the evening together. After a swift foray to the kitchen he returned with a tea-towel wrapped, turban fashion, about his balding grey head. Seizing upon a deck of cards he expanded and collapsed it as if it were a concertina.

'Henrietta, my dear,' Ashton boomed, 'select a card. Any card. Glance at it. Yes, you may show it to Elaine. Now, put it back. Anywhere . . . that's fine. Now, Mrs. Brokaw, if you will shuffle the pack. As much as you wish — '

Lambie Pie giggled, mixed the cards sloppily and returned them.

Ashton's thick fingers and generally bumbling movements made it appear that he might be more proficient at laying brick than in performing minor miracles, but his homely face held a benign glow. A few awkward passes and he triumphantly held up the queen of hearts.

Henrietta, Elaine and Lambie Pie gasped in unison, but Cissie Folwell was not to be upstaged.

'I saw Bill Donath yesterday.' Cissie's voice could summon a maid from any point within her twenty-room house. 'He was drunk, gutter drunk. Looked as if he'd been that way for days.'

Lyman Ashton, looking slightly foolish in his tea-towel turban, abruptly sat down. Wick grinned mirthlessly, and Arthur Brokaw's usually good-natured face was lumpy and ugly. Christopher, holding a cup brimful of steaming coffee, got up and quietly moved behind Cissie's chair.

'I suppose everyone ought to sympathize with him,' Cissie delicately speared a pickle, 'since Marge ran out on him the way she did. Or did she? What a perfectly divine scandal! I think it's the strangest thing the way they managed to keep the other woman's name out of it. But do you know what I heard? I heard — '

Henrietta's scream was fractionally ahead of Cissie's, but it was immediately smothered in pitch and volume. Ashton stood stunned and gaping, and it was Wick who summoned presence of mind enough to snatch the tea-towel and attempt to repair some of the damage that Christopher's coffee had done to Cissie's lap.

★   ★   ★

It was all very simple, or so it had seemed.

You were an architect and in the course of your work you had met an interior decorator. Your ideas seemed to harmonize with hers and you got along quite well. You discovered that she was living alone, and lonely, and so when you had finished work you sometimes took her to dinner. It became a sort of oasis, this business of having dinner with her. And then it was but a step further to her apartment. Admittedly her apartment was a nicer place to work of an evening than a draughty, cluttered office from which everyone else had gone home. And then one evening you didn't feel like working; that is, perhaps you felt like it but the ideas just wouldn't co-operate. So she found a bottle of scotch, and then you discovered that she was fond of the *Warsaw Concerto* and Bach and Benny Goodman, and that she liked to dance with her shoes off. And then you forgot about work; forgot —

It was as simple as that.

Christopher turned into Echo Road.

The first white house after passing the bend beyond the bridge, she had said. He knew the place. It stood in a little clearing, the only house in the valley visible from Lyman Ashton's terrace. Lyman had considered it before the place on the Ridge became available; he had wanted to be higher up or something, so he had bought on the Ridge.

Odd, that he had met both Lyman and Ruth at the same time, although they hadn't been together. He had met them at the Donaths, while it was still 'the Donaths' and not just another house. That was at least eight months ago and Bill had just sold Lyman Ashton the place on the Ridge. 'He's a swell gent, a writer. Been everywhere. Want everybody to meet him.' That had been Bill. And Ruth had been a college friend of Marge's. 'Look out, Chris. She's dynamite!' That had been Marge.

'Ruth Cassell, I want you to meet Chris Elliot. Isn't he beautiful? Bend down a little, gorgeous!'

She had seemed so bored, aloof and alone. Bill had a new gadget for making records and everyone was talking into it with Lyman Ashton acting as impromptu master of ceremonies. She hadn't gone for the idea much, or for Ashton either. Christopher had talked with her, and that was when he found out that she was an interior decorator, working in town for a firm he knew quite well; she'd been there right along and he'd never noticed her.

That was how it had started.

Perhaps it was fitting. The cycle of fate. It was the Donaths who had brought them together and it was the Donaths, or rather the sickening news of them, that had brought Christopher to his senses. What had he, with so much at stake — what in heaven's name had he been thinking of?

And tonight, in order to come to her, he had lied once again. He had told Henrietta that if Bill Donath, the son of his old partner, was gutter drunk somewhere then it was his duty to find him and bring him home.

Disintegration. That was how it started. Little things piling up into slow decay.

First the problem, then the bottle, then the gutter.

It was a one-way street.

'I'll tell her,' he promised himself as the white cottage came in view. 'I'll tell her straight and plain. She knew I was married, and a father. Thank heaven I never tried to hide that.'

* * *

She had been reading or dozing, or possibly she might have been crying, for her eyes were misty and just the least bit swollen. She was without shoes, and as Christopher followed her across a dinky foyer and into a box-like living room he thought, 'This isn't going to be easy.'

She hadn't made any attempt at an emotional display; hadn't tried to throw herself in his arms or kiss him or cling to his hand. She had appeared only relieved and genuinely glad to see him, and for that he was thankful.

In the centre of the room she turned about and quick amusement lighted her face. 'Oh, for heaven's sake,' she laughed.

'Take off your coat! Here, sit down and I'll mix a drink. Anyone might think you'd come to sell me insurance!'

Christopher removed his topcoat, folded it carefully and with studied precision laid it over a chair. 'Well,' he said, and gingerly sat down on another chair.

She was in the kitchen, rattling glasses and ice trays. 'Like my little house?' she called out to him.

Christopher glanced around. 'It's quite a house,' he replied. That seemed inadequate so he hastily added, 'I've often noticed it. This house is the only one you can see clearly from Lyman Ashton's — he's up on the Ridge. So many trees on Echo Road, you know. Echo *Valley* Road is the proper name, I believe — ' He swallowed.

She came to the door of the room and stood regarding him. Her face, he saw, was curiously mottled. 'Lyman Ashton, did you say? You mean the writer? Where did you say he lived?'

'Up on the Ridge. You can probably see his house from your back porch. You must remember Ashton; he's the one the Donaths gave the party for, the time I met you. Ashton was the homely fellow with all the personality; must be fifty, anyway.'

'Oh, yes. I remember,' she answered faintly and returned to the kitchen.

Christopher was annoyed. Wasn't it just like a woman to attend a party and not know for whom it was given? He wondered if he should tell her that Ashton had been interested in this house and would probably have bought it if the one on the Ridge hadn't suddenly become available. And then he thought: 'Why bother? It made no difference anyway.'

She came in, bearing two tall glasses. She had taken advantage of the interval to repair her make-up and she looked a lot less forlorn. She handed him a glass, smiled down at him and then went to curl up on the divan.

'It's nice to see you,' she said. She made a toast of it by lifting her glass.

The nearness of her warmth and smile made Christopher tense again. Putting his drink down untasted he glanced directly at her and said, 'Ruth, this is very awkward. It is difficult for me to say what I must, and I wish it were not necessary for me to say it.'

'If it's as bad as all that, don't.' She smiled at him across the rim of her glass. 'Why be mid-Victorian? You're really a nice person, Chris.'

The greyness returned to his cheeks. 'Please don't make it more difficult. My sole reason for coming here tonight was to tell you that I can't see you again. You must understand that. You know my position. I know that it was wrong and so do you. We simply can't go on.'

She was still smiling, as if amused at some inner secret, but the mottled hue had returned to her skin. 'Why can't we? What's wrong, dear? Have the Donaths and their domestic difficulties got you down?'

'If it weren't that, it would be something else. You know very well such things can't last. If we kept it up we would only destroy each other.'

She raised her glass and drank long and

deliberately. She brought it down and a little of the liquid spilled from her lips and down over her chin. She looked at him with eyes that had become hard hot points in circles of white.

'Why, Chris?' she demanded. 'Why should anything have changed between us? There's nothing unnatural or abnormal in our relationship. Until two weeks ago, until you stopped coming to see me, stopped altogether without a word, we were happy, normal people. We gave to each other and we benefited. There was nothing sordid about it. The sordidness is only something that has come between us because of someone else. I haven't got in your way, Chris. I haven't demanded too much. I only ask now that we can work together and play together sometimes as we have in the past. I've never asked you to leave your wife or give up your home for me. I've never asked you for anything; I have only given. You say we would destroy each other. Why? Do you want to destroy me?'

'Really, Ruth, I don't know what to say

to you. Can't you understand that I'm married and that I have two children whose home and happiness are more important to me than anything in the world? Can't you see what effect this will have on them when it eventually comes out, as it must?'

'Why must it come out?'

'In heaven's name, Ruth! No one, not even I, knew that Bill Donath had been carrying on an affair; even now — no one knows who the woman was. But look what it has done to him!'

She turned her face away. 'You were just as much married and just as much a father when you started this thing. Why didn't you think this way then?'

Christopher fisted his hands. 'You knew. Why did you let me?'

She faced him again. He had expected to see tears, but of them there was no trace. She sighed, drank a long swallow until only ice remained and, lifting the glass in a gesture of finality, said, 'Well, I guess that's that.'

Relieved, Christopher fidgeted to go. 'I'm sorry to be so harsh, but I'm glad

I've finally made you see it my way — the right way.'

She glanced at him with brief, returning amusement. 'Honestly, Chris, you're priceless. You sound just like something out of Sheridan.' Leaning her head back she laughed. There was no hint of hysteria; the laugh came from deep within some secret well of amusement.

'What's so funny?' Christopher demanded, nettled.

'I was thinking of how little you know about me, or about other women. I was thinking also of your wife.' She brought her head down and regarded him with mirth-filled eyes. 'I never told you, did I, that she came to see me — yes, she did. It was no more than a month ago. She visited my apartment one evening and I don't yet know whether or not she was surprised not to find you there. We had a nice, civil chat; very civil. She talked mostly about you and the children. By the way, there was a man with her. He didn't come in, though; he remained in the car.'

A man. It was probably Wick. Had

Henrietta really called at Ruth's apartment, or was this just a sample of sour grapes? 'I'm sorry, but I really must go. It's quite late you know.'

'Of course it is. How inconsiderate of me. Of course you must go.'

He arose awkwardly. 'If there's anything I can do — '

'There is. Yes, there is.' Her eyes sought the bottom of her glass, and her fingers clutched it tightly. 'You can go. Quickly, please.'

Christopher gathered his coat and hat and without saying goodnight, went out.

The night was clear, drenched in moonlight. Small things stood out sharply. The straggling privet bushes. A grey mass of rock on the opposite side of the road. A lonely, drunken telephone pole. A white-painted sign warning of the curve in the road.

In the far distance a dog howled, received an answer, and the duet died on the fitful breeze. High on the Ridge the windows of Lyman Ashton's solitary house gave back vacant moon glow. The valley in which he stood, with its winding road and shroud of trees, seemed an unreal world.

Christopher, as he fitted ignition key to lock, discovered that his hand was shaking violently.

★　★　★

As he came up the street, Christopher saw that his house was ablaze with light. Two cars were parked in the driveway, one Wick's and one of them strange, and he had to manoeuvre carefully to pass them. As he parked his heart sank and with a rush of memory he recalled what he had done to Cissie Folwell. He was not sorry for his act; if he had felt even the slightest remorse, he had quickly dismissed it after the scene she'd made. But with Wick here it could mean anything. As much as Wick hated his employer and might secretly enjoy seeing her discomfited, he hated Christopher more. And Wick was wise. Christopher might have successfully fooled Henrietta for the past half year, but he hadn't fooled Wick.

Slowly he forced his dragging footsteps to cover the brick-pathed terrace while he tried to think of some excuse; an alibi for his recent absence. He'd told Henrietta that he was going out to look for Bill Donath, but that was no good. Wick would likely know where Bill was, had probably gone in search of him the minute he'd seen Elaine home.

Christopher could think of nothing to say when he entered his house and found Wick waiting, sitting stiffly in the chair at the foot of the stairs.

Wick jumped up. 'I waited because I wanted to tell you this myself,' he announced coldly. 'Your daughter Christina has a streptococcic throat infection. She is running a very high temperature, a hundred and six according to Doctor Slade. Thus far your son seems to have escaped the infection and I've taken him to my home so that his grandmother can look after him. I'd appreciate it if you would insist that Henrietta get some rest; she refuses to allow a nurse to come in. If there's nothing further to be done here, I'll be going.'

* * *

At six in the morning it was Agnes who finally prevailed upon Christopher to take a shower, shave himself, and 'drink some of this coffee I've been making and eat some of these eggs before they get stone cold. And go to work! You're no use around here; sickness is a woman's job. The little girl'll be all right, now; she's got the best help there is. Will you *get*?'

* * *

He made a train a full hour earlier than was his custom. He hoped that the chance of his taking it might help him to avoid Ruth. But it did not. He had scarcely found a seat when she entered the coach.

Ruth walked toward him and directly by, either not seeing or ignoring him, to disappear into the coach behind.

2

The offices of Donath and Elliot occupied the second floor front of an old brownstone located within a two-block radius of the central railway terminal. Here were heart and arteries of the city's commerce; during the day these narrow streets washed with the ebb and flow of people and vehicles; during the night they were gloomy ill-lighted canyons, the scuttleways of human rodents, tainted with the odour of the slums of which they were so nearly a part.

There was no longer a Donath in the firm. Theodore, the founder (he had been Bill's father) had died some five years before, and Christopher had purchased his share from the estate. The price had been steep but the firm was well known, the business extensive and the profits such that in less than another year he would be completely free of debt.

This morning, an hour earlier than his

usual time, Christopher experienced no particular satisfaction in noting that all the draughtsmen were already busily at work. Perhaps it was fitting that Margaret was ten minutes late, and this fact did not deter her from spending an additional ten minutes in the completion of her toilette. Margaret was receptionist, stenographer, bookkeeper, chancellor of the petty cash and postage fund, keeper of the stock-room and mother-confessor of the flock. She was also known to practically every builder in town as 'The Rock', and she was the only person in the world of whom Christopher was a little in awe.

Without removing hat or topcoat he sat at his desk and pulled a stack of work towards him, and even as he busied himself he knew exactly what Margaret would say to him. He looked mouldy as last year's mince pie. When was he going to start earning the supervisory fees on the Claypoole job? The new man, Griggs, couldn't tell the difference between shiplap siding and page twelve of the Farmer's Almanac. Somebody ought to give Cohen at Plumbing Supply merry

hell about the chromium fixtures speci-
fied for the Trentino Building. Had he
seen the blueprints that had been coming
through lately? Well, had he tried to read
one?

He stopped turning the typed pages of
specifications, scowled at a paragraph and
reached for a pencil. Wetting the point of
it he bracketed the paragraph heavily and
in the margin wrote *Specify Blue Giant
Cement on all jobs!*

There was nothing wrong with Blue
Giant cement, and it was nobody's
business but his own that he got a
rake-off of a nickel a bag.

Laying the specification to one side he
saw that Margaret had finally completed
her own architecture and was at her
morning inspection of work in progress.
No one, apparently, had told her yet that
he was in the office.

Hastily he scribbled a note that he
would be out all day, and then he fled via
the men's lavatory. When he was in the
hall, trying to decide whether to wait for
the lift or use the stairs, he glanced back
and the thought came to him that instead

of *Donath and Elliot* the legend of the door should read *Margaret O'Bannigan*.

It was Margaret who ran the business.

* * *

As the five-ten pulled out of the terminal, Christopher was occupying an aisle seat about midway of the coach. He had returned to the office at a late hour and had found several notes to call Ruth. Margaret had handed them to him amongst a batch of other stuff. He was surprised. He had thought that the issue was quite clear. He had felt that because of last night's visit an understanding had been reached. When Ruth had passed him on the train this morning it had been evident that she desired to avoid him. What could she possibly want to say to him now?

He folded his newspaper lengthwise and tried to find in it something other than divorce news. Newspapers are notably uncooperative. If you suffer a heart ailment there is nothing to be read but news of sudden deaths from heart disease. If you know an unfortunate fellow who has absconded, every third item is about embezzlement. If you are worried about your stocks, the financial news is bound to be alarming. If you have to make a business trip by plane, the news columns are certain to be filled with airplane crashes.

Margaret had told him that Teena would get over it. What, outside of practically everything about the building business, did Margaret know? Christopher had called home five times during the day; the last time Agnes had sounded mad. 'Listen, Mr. Elliot, we got other things to do than answer the telephone every ten minutes. Her fever's down, yes, the doctor's been here, no, Mrs. Elliot still won't get a nurse. No, there isn't anything we want from town. My good lands!'

Agnes probably thought it strange that he should be so concerned; there had been times when he had neglected to call to say that he wouldn't be home for supper. Perhaps Henrietta thought it was strange, too. He and Henrietta had agreed to the same set of rules. She had stuck by them, but what had happened to him?

The rules of marriage didn't always coincide with the rules of nature. If you'd had to drive for an education, drive for a job, survival, recognition, advancement, success, you'd had no time to realize the demands nature made of you. Cumulative demands, slowly building like the compression of a spring.

There were men whom Christopher knew who said the hell with it and went at it with their eyes open; got themselves some tramp and put her in an apartment and charged her mink coat and other upkeep to institutional expenses. You couldn't exactly call it infidelity, either. If they had remained poor they would probably have remained faithful; they had outgrown their wives just as surely as they had outgrown coffee and doughnut lunches, small furnished flats and ready-made suits. With Christopher Elliot it was different. He had married above his station and he knew it, despite the fact he was deeply fond of Henrietta. What had happened to him was that he had just gone along kidding himself until one day —

An item in the newspaper about a little boy aged two who was being flown to Baltimore for treatment to combat streptococcic infection. It was hoped that Doctor (unpronounceable name) of Johns Hopkins would be able to save his life.

Christopher drove from the station to his garage in slightly under three minutes, and before his car had stopped rolling he was running for the house.

★　★　★

It had never occurred to him that in any sort of real crisis he might be apt to lose his head. He had been through emergencies, some of them extremely trying. He had survived financial reverses, conducting himself with a cheerful courage that drew admiration from those who knew his actual circumstances. He had become known as a cool, clever and sometimes ruthless operator. He had learned that more than creative ability was required of him; he had also to be able to handle people, to kindle enthusiasm in them. He felt that the people who worked with him, and the people with whom he did business, had to be convinced of his infallibility. He had accomplished this so well he had become convinced of it himself.

He did not know how utterly helpless he could be until he was faced with the sickness of a child.

Henrietta performed her ministrations with masterful and unruffled serenity, betraying by not so much as the drooping of an eyelid that she might be tired or fed up. Christopher fretted a great deal and got in the way, but Henrietta's usual efficiency was so increased that he was sometimes hard put to realize that in an upstairs bedroom was the sick, fretful and bored little person who was his daughter.

There were none of the accepted evidences of sickness about the house. No mess in bathroom or kitchen, no pans or bottles, no odour of medicines. Teena was fed, bathed, doctored and bedded without fuss or ostentation. Within a few days

Christopher's first panic had worn off. When he got to see his daughter, which by arrangement was just before dinner and at prayer time, she looked little different to him than she did when well. There was a fresh supply of magazines by his favourite chair, beer and snacks in the refrigerator, plenty of cigarettes and solitude. He could not have had as good service at the City Club.

But with it all, Henrietta was distant and aloof. He had laid it at first to her concern for Teena, but now he wasn't so sure.

There were occasional visitors. The Brokaws made a perfunctory call in which Arthur hinted at a big job he would soon have. Lyman Ashton brought Elaine Loring and they remained until it was obvious that they were going on to join Wick and Cissie Folwell somewhere else. Wickie came with Grandmother Geer and after the first joyous tussle the event turned flat.

He brought work home to do. He had been spending little time in his office because he feared the moment might arrive when Ruth would tire of telephoning and appear for a scene. He took over the supervision of several jobs and the change in routine helped him a little.

It was late in the evening of the fourth day of Teena's illness. It was Sunday, and beyond going out for newspapers and a brief walk, he had spent all of it in checking over a mass of detail drawings.

He sat in his study, completely absorbed, so that he did not immediately notice the ringing of the telephone.

Annoyed because the telephone was not answered, and because the ringing did not stop, Christopher glanced at his watch to discover that the hour was past midnight. He realized also that he was very tired, and as he rose he rubbed the nape of his neck and flexed his shoulders.

He had reached the hall when he heard Henrietta on the stair landing. She called down to him, 'Chris? I thought you were in bed. I was so surprised when I — will you answer it? I've got to look in at Teena. She wakened as usual.'

Christopher seized the phone. Angrily

he said, 'One of these days we're either going to have this bell changed or — hello? Hello, who is this? Who is speaking?'

The answering voice seemed at first scarcely human. Incoherent, choked with sobbing; an admixture of fear and relief and a release of long-contained emotions.

'It sounds like a drunk,' Christopher announced wrathfully. 'Who are you and what do you want?'

Hysteria. A sobbing intake of breath that sent chills down his spine. And then, rushed but more understandable, 'Chris, if I ever meant anything to you, you will come to me now. Now! Don't you understand? I need you — oh, dear God, please let me — '

'You're drunk,' Christopher said shortly.

Henrietta left the landing and moved along the hall because Teena had started to cry.

'*Drunk*? I hate you. I loathe and despise you — oh, Chris, I need you! If you don't come to me now I'm coming to your house. To your house! Do you hear me? I can't stay here another moment — '

She broke off into violent and uncontrolled sobbing. He heard a sharp sound, a *chock*, and for a second he thought she had closed the connection. But then he heard the noise of running footsteps and the slam of a door.

He didn't know what to think, or what to do. As if in a trance he replaced the telephone and simply stood. His heart seemed to stop beating; he could not breathe; his tongue threatened to strangle him.

Henrietta returned to the stair landing. She was more awake now. 'Teena's — ' she began. She looked down at him and gave a little cry. 'What's wrong, Chris? Are you ill?'

He could not answer.

She came down a step. 'What is it? What's wrong? I heard you say something about a drunk. Was it Bill Donath? Is he in trouble?'

'Trouble?' Christopher's voice was a harsh croak.

She came the rest of the way down. She had put on a robe over her nightgown and her feet were shod in the beaded white doeskin moccasins he had bought for her in Montreal.

She was still slightly flushed from sleep. She stood a moment, glancing anxiously at him, and then her gaze wavered and fell. Sighing, she turned away. 'I suppose you'd better go to him,' she said in a dead voice.

★　★　★

It was not above a mile and a half to the cottage on Echo Road and Christopher had little time to organize his thoughts. Fear lent him recklessness and he drove fast, too fast for safety. Above all he did not want Ruth to come to his home; Henrietta must not find out about him in this way.

If only things hadn't been so confused. If only he had been able to face Henrietta when he wasn't under such great obligation to her. He had honestly intended to tell her; confess, explain or whatever it amounted to, but Teena's illness had lost him the opportunity and there had been no chance since. And now, if Ruth should come to his house in a drunken or hysterical condition — Christopher shuddered.

As he shot into Echo Road he realized that he was driving much too fast. For an agonized moment he lost control and his car swayed from side to side of the narrow, twisting way. There was a jarring scrape as he brushed the fence guarding the culvert on the wrong side of the road, and had there been another vehicle approaching at that moment Christopher Elliot's problems would have been of another sort and out of his hands for a long time.

Somehow he made it. Grimly roused and thoroughly shaken he regained the right side and had slowed to safer speed when he reached the narrow bridge.

On the stage that his headlights made of the bridge he saw Ruth running blindly toward him.

For a disturbing instant Christopher experienced the savage desire to kill; to run her down, to smash and leave her lying there. When he had stopped and she had reached the side of the car, he was trembling almost as violently as she.

★　★　★

She had thrown a brown tweed coat over her pyjamas, and though she might have had on some sort of footwear when she started from the cottage, her feet were now bare. In the dim light of the dash lamp he saw that they were scratched and bleeding. Her hands, too, were scraped and her chin was cut. All along her left side, extending over her face and even to her hair, were particles of leaves and dirt and bits of twigs as if she had fallen headlong.

He tried to get some sense out of her, to make her incoherent babbling stop, but she seemed not to want to talk to him. She drew away and crouched sobbing in her corner of the seat. She kept her face averted and her injured hands were fisted and tightly held against her breasts.

When she realized that he was driving her back to the cottage she cried out violently, 'No!' and fought him for possession of the wheel.

Christopher jammed on the brakes, fended her off and then roughly grasped her hands. 'Do you want to wreck us? Stop it!' he commanded. 'Get control of yourself!'

She would not cease struggling. 'Please don't take me back there. Please don't take me — '

Suddenly he released her hands and in a swift movement grabbed her by the shoulders. Shaking her, he cried, 'Ruth!' sharply.

For an instant her crazy, fear-filled eyes rested on his. Her face was mottled, almost purple. Her lips were tightly drawn against her teeth and the cut in her chin showed black. She was utterly rigid, and then abruptly the fight went out of her. Her head rolled and she sagged against his hands.

'Oh, Chris,' she moaned. 'How can you be so cruel to me?'

'Cruel? If you don't mind, I'd like to know what this is all about. I was under the impression that we had reached an understanding. What's happened? What's wrong with you?'

'You didn't answer one of my calls — don't you realize that I wouldn't come to you, that nothing could make me, if I didn't need you? And tonight — tonight you said I was drunk — oh, how I despise you — ' She began to sob, a dry, wracking sound that raised hackles at the back of Christopher's neck.

'All right, Ruth. I'm sorry. I didn't know what to think. I still don't. But you've got to be sensible. I'll drive you to your cottage, and then you can explain all this business.'

Her head came up. 'Please, Chris — don't leave me. Don't make me stay there alone. I couldn't bear it. Please say you won't!'

Christopher made no answer. He had worked himself into a fine rage and was prepared to ride roughshod over what he thought was a trick, or if not a trick then some hallucination of her hysterical state. When he had heard her on the telephone he had been convinced that she had drunk herself into an alcoholic frenzy. But now he knew she had not been drinking at all. And after seeing the terror in her eyes he did not know what to think. He had never seen anyone in her condition, or in a condition even approaching it.

He began to be a little frightened himself.

They reached the cottage and pulled into the driveway. There were lights on in the house and he was glad for the sense of sanity they gave him. He switched off his engine and cut his headlights.

There was no moon, but a faint starlight distorted familiar objects. The winding road looked like a river. The hedge loomed larger than it should have been; the white cottage seemed detached, floating in air. The tree appeared to be reaching down as if reluctant to leave the security of the ground.

He turned to her. 'Give me your key.'

The presence of the cottage, or whatever it was that she had fled, set the chill of silence on her. She shook her head.

His gorge started to rise, and then he understood. Of course. Silly woman: she had dashed out, leaving handbag and key within the house. The door was equipped with a spring lock and so they were locked out. Suddenly suspicious, Christopher asked, 'Is there someone inside? Answer me, damn it! I'm trying to help you. You've got to co-operate.'

Shaking her head, she spoke reluctantly. 'No one is in there.'

The way she said it made him look at her with narrowing eyes, and a new suspicion formed in his brain. He wondered if she might suddenly and unaccountably have gone mad.

'Well, I'm going in.' The loudness of his voice startled him. 'If I can't find an open window I'll break one. I intend to get this business settled for once and all.'

He opened the door to step out, and with a little cry she clung to him.

He was impatient. 'Don't be ridiculous! You have no shoes on your feet, and you're only half dressed. Stay in the car. I'll get in some way and open the front door, and then I'll call you.'

But she would not budge from his side. Exhaling in exasperation he stepped out and she scrambled after him. She caught at his sleeve and clung tightly to him, so hampering his movements that in climbing the steps to the rear porch he stumbled and nearly fell.

The door was securely fastened. It was a stock four-light affair, and he supposed it to be an inch and five-eighths in thickness and probably fitted with three butts in addition to both a common and a spring lock. He wasted neither time nor effort in trying to force it. Roughly thrusting the girl aside he put his back to the door. Raising his left elbow to the centre of a glass panel he made a fist of his left hand and struck it sharply with his right.

The glass fell in with a tinkling crash.

It was dark in the shadow of the porch and before he had removed sufficient glass fragments to permit him to reach through he had cut his right palm badly. Swearing, he unlocked the door from the inside and opened it. Entering the kitchen he found the panel switch, turned on the light and then examined his hand.

It was bleeding profusely from a diagonal cut an inch and a half in length.

He went to the sink and turned cold water into his palm, letting the water run over onto his wrist. When the bleeding had slowed he whipped out a handkerchief and turned peremptorily to Ruth.

'Here, help me — '

His voice died. He had seen her only in dim light before. He was genuinely shocked now. After his first startled glance he avoided looking at her. With his left hand he clumsily tied the handkerchief himself.

He said, briskly, 'I'll stay with you while you clean yourself up. And you'd better get into something warmer.'

She wasn't listening to him. Unmindful of the jagged glass on the floor, she had walked across and at the entrance of the living room had paused to look back at him. There was something subdued, almost hypnotic in her actions.

Because of the damage to his hand he had forgotten her momentarily, and now it was the wound he forgot. Uneasily he followed her. As they entered the living room he heard a buzzing sound; he was mystified until he identified it as the dial tone of the telephone she had dropped in her flight. He went over to it and replaced the instrument on its prongs. His sharp, searching glance swept the room and he saw nothing that he had not seen on his previous visit.

He was bewildered. 'Say, what is all this?' he demanded

She was standing in the doorway of the bedroom, staring in fascination at her bed. With rapid strides he passed by her, stopped in the centre of the small room and looked about. He saw nothing but a rumpled bed, clothing draped on a chair, and litter on the dressing table. Puzzled, he sought her eyes and then he turned to follow the line of her sight.

Angrily he strode to the bed and snatched at an object on the pillow.

'A dead mouse!' he exclaimed. 'Well, I'm damned! Now I've seen everything!'

★ ★ ★

'Ruth, I ought to break your neck.' He was shaking with rage. 'I don't know what to say to you. Do you mean to tell me that you called me out of my house after midnight, that you made me come down here, and that you ran from this place practically naked and screaming in terror all because of a mouse? What sort of miserable trick is this?'

His anger fanned a spark within her. She had been hysterical; fascinated and terrified at the same time. Now she was only tired and soiled and pale.

'Chris, I tried a dozen times to call you at your office.' She spoke in a low voice, and in deadly earnest. 'I didn't want to call you at your home because I knew how you would feel about it. I didn't want to, but tonight I had to. There was nothing else for me to do. For the past week, ever since the last time I saw you, there has been a man watching my apartment. I thought at first he might be someone you had employed.'

She raised her hand wearily to brush the hair from her eyes. She saw then, apparently for the first time, that her hand was badly bruised. She saw too, or rather felt, that this was not the extent of her hurts. Angrily she shrugged off weakness.

'Then I thought, no. You wouldn't do such a thing. There was no reason for it. But your wife might. Your wife might want evidence, so I tried to warn you in case you should change your mind about — about coming to see me. But you didn't answer any of my calls, so I didn't care. At that time I hadn't started being afraid.'

She inhaled deeply and pulled the brown coat tighter about her. She swayed a little. 'Would you mind,' she asked unsteadily, 'getting me a drink? You'll find scotch in the cupboard above the sink. Mix one for yourself if you want to, but I'd like mine straight.

He would have brushed the request aside. His anger knew no bounds, but there was something about her rigid control that held him. Wordless, he went to the kitchen, found bottle and glass and brought them back. He poured a stiff jolt for her and stood back while she drank it in a single swallow.

She coughed a little. She handed him

the glass, but she did not again ask him to help himself. She said, 'Four nights ago I discovered that this man was not only watching my apartment; he was also following me. I wasn't frightened; in spite of what you may think, I don't frighten easily. But I was annoyed. I told George, the janitor, about it. George is a nice person; he does little things for me — He went out looking for the man. After a while he came up to my apartment and reported that he hadn't been able to spot anyone hanging around, but he would keep watch.

'The thing went on. This man continued to follow me, but I couldn't catch him. I couldn't get close enough see him, although I tried enough times. He was too clever. He was always a shadow among other shadows.'

She lifted her head and looked levelly at Christopher. 'I know what you're thinking. You think I was imagining things; that I was jumping at shadows. I might have thought so too if he hadn't telephoned me.' She shuddered and her head dropped down. 'I shall never forget his voice. He told me I was cute, and that he liked the way I wiggled when I walked, and he said that I shouldn't be afraid of him. He asked me if I would mind being nice to him, and when I didn't answer he hung up.'

She sighed and said, 'Give me just a little more. I'm almost through now.'

Christopher poured a drink, and when she had returned the glass this time he poured one for himself. His anger had cooled, abating to curiosity. 'What did you do then?' he asked.

'Oh, I tried tracing the call, but it was no good. You can't get anywhere with a dial telephone. I notified the telephone company and they said they would put a monitor on my calls, but he must have known about that because he didn't try again. I hadn't meant to come back here to Chelmere except to pack my clothes, but because of him I came, thinking I might be safe here. There was only one place where I seemed to be able to shake him. Do you remember that awful beanery on Ward Avenue where you took me the first night we worked late together?' He avoided her eyes. 'I think so. You mean the one about halfway between our offices?'

She nodded as if impatient at the interruption. 'I discovered that you could walk through the restaurant and come into an alley leading to C Street. On C Street you have your choice of going down to the railway terminal or up to Grant Avenue. I managed to lose him there, so I was fairly sure he didn't know about my having a cottage in Chelmere. That is,' she breathed in quickly, 'I was until tonight.'

'Tonight I read for a while and went to bed about ten. I sleep well, once I get started. I had felt fairly secure; nothing had happened to make me feel otherwise. The telephone had rung once, at about eight o'clock: a woman was soliciting for a drive of some kind. I was sleeping soundly when it rang again — '

She paused and looked around. 'I've simply got to sit down,' she said.

Christopher followed her to the divan. As she drew her feet up he shuddered with revulsion at their filth. His reaction did not escape her attention, but she misinterpreted it.

'I'm almost finished,' she said wearily. 'When I'm through, if you'll just stand by while I pack a few things, and then take me to the bus ... The telephone woke me at midnight. I couldn't imagine who it could be; for the moment I had completely forgotten about *him*. I got up and answered, and then I heard something I hope I shall never hear again. It was the crying of a cat.'

Christopher gaped. 'On the telephone?' he asked incredulously.

'On the telephone. I listened, at first annoyed, then angry, and finally, scared. I put the receiver back and returned to the bedroom. It was then I saw the mouse. I don't know if the mouse was there when I got up to answer the phone; it might have been. I only know it was there, on the pillow, when I returned. It was just a hands-breadth from where my head had been.'

Suddenly she covered her face with her

bruised hands. 'Oh, Chris,' she sobbed. 'Why would anyone do this awful thing to me?'

3

Christopher Elliot was possessed of a logical brain. He could believe in the results of arithmetic because he could add, subtract, multiply and divide. He did not argue that a straight line might not be the shortest distance between two points; he dealt in lines. There were a great many things he could accept because he could divine the logic that made them so.

He could not take the shadowy figure of an unknown plus the telephoned meowing of a cat plus a deceased white mouse and add them into any sensible sum. His logical brain told him that such things simply did not happen.

Attractive and unattended girls were frequently followed. The follower might be a love-sick swain. Or he might be a professional who was being paid for spying, or else a footpad or a maniac. That part was unfortunate, but it was at least understandable.

But the incredible business of cat and mouse!

He did not know what to think. Beyond any question he knew that Ruth was frightened. She was ill and bordering on collapse. In her unreasoning flight she had added physical distress to the mental torment she was suffering. After she had calmed down she had told her story in a simple, direct and unaffected way. She had spoken as one might reasonably be expected to speak in telling the truth.

But a cat on the telephone!

Unceremoniously, Christopher buried the mouse in the flush bowl. While Ruth was washing and dressing he made an inspection of the house. He even went as far as the cellar which he hastily left because it was damp and cobwebby and it did not look as if anyone had been down there for a long time. He wasn't sure just what he was searching for. He searched partly because he felt it was expected of him, and partly because by so doing he might appease Ruth by giving at least outward credence to story.

He found nothing to either substantiate

or disprove her. He had a growing suspicion that the whole affair was an invention designed to force him back to her through pity or curiosity. He knew it was possible for people to work themselves into hysteria and in the process imagine things which they truly believed to be real. The business of Ruth's falling: according to psychologists, people were sometimes 'accident-prone' because they were starved for attention. In this she might easily be the victim of her subconscious mind.

But that would not explain away the mouse.

No woman in her right mind would kill a mouse, put it on her pillow and then run screaming away, barefoot through hedgerow and over rock gully on a cold autumn night. And mice just didn't die on pillows; they died in walls or under floors and sometimes their passing created a minor construction problem.

Christopher did not know what to think, but there was one thing of which he was sure. In her present state Ruth was dangerous. He must take her to the bus. He would recommend that she visit a psychiatrist. And that, regardless, must be the end so far as he was concerned.

She appeared in the doorway of the bedroom. She was fully dressed and had brushed her brown tweed coat so that it was a bit more presentable. Her face was heavily made up so that the area of damage on her chin was not too noticeable, and she had covered her hands with gloves. But there remained a discoloration on the left side of her face, extending from cheekbone to temple, which no amount of powder could hide, and she looked altogether washed out and ill.

'I'm ready,' she announced in a listless voice.

Christopher took the small overnight case from her. 'I don't know anything about the buses,' he confessed worriedly, 'but there should be one. I believe they run every hour or so.'

'It doesn't matter.' She passed by him, limping as she walked, turning out lights. 'I suppose we'll have to leave the kitchen door as it is — perhaps I'd better lock it anyway.'

They went out by the front door, and in the path between the scraggly hedgerows his foot struck an object. He picked it up; it was one of her slippers.

'What — '

She was already in the car. Shrugging, he dropped the slipper behind the hedge and followed.

★   ★   ★

He could not bring himself to mention a psychiatrist. He supposed he should ask questions, so he commenced with, 'Can you think of anyone who would want to persecute you for any reason?'

Apparently she was not listening to him. She was occupied in glancing idly at the path of the headlights, watching trees disappear in darkness while she immersed herself in private thoughts.

He touched her. 'Do you know who might have been responsible for this business?'

Her head turned apathetically. 'Your wife might.'

He glared. 'Henrietta? Don't be absurd! She's been in bed all evening.'

'She might have hired someone.'

His face became stern. 'I think you're being very unfair. If you knew Henrietta at all you'd know she was incapable of such a thing. Besides, despite the fact you told me she had visited you at your apartment, I don't believe she knows about us. Not at all.'

'She knows.'

He shrugged impatiently. 'Last week you told me I didn't know very much about you. What is there to know?'

'Not much, really.' She smiled faintly. 'I am an illegitimate daughter of a king. Prior to meeting you I was a President's mistress.'

'Don't try to be funny! Can't you see what I'm driving at? If there's any truth in the story you told me tonight, there must be someone behind it. Perhaps some person from your past — '

'If there's any truth!' she blazed. 'I suppose you think I've arranged all that's happened to me just so I could get your sympathy. Oh, such colossal conceit! If I were a man I'd knock you down!'

'We'll get nowhere by saying nasty things to each other. I'm sorry if my choice of words was inept. Please try to think. Can you think of anyone who might go to such lengths to annoy you?'

'I don't want to talk to you. I shouldn't have called you; I should have called the police. How do I know it wasn't you? You're through with me. You've sent me on my way, but I haven't gone. As long as I remain either here or in town I'm a source of embarrassment to you. You're shrewd and clever and unscrupulous enough — '

'Ruth! Stop it!'

She turned away and looked out the window. Presently her tension passed and her head dropped and she began to cry softly.

He turned the car out of Echo Road and street lights appeared. They would soon reach the bus station and despite the lateness of the hour they would be sure to run into someone. He did not want a scene.

He glanced aside anxiously. 'Ruth, please. I know I've acted very badly. I don't blame you for despising me. I've said a lot of things that I shouldn't, but can't you see that I'm upset? This thing affects me in a way as much as it does you. I'd like to know who or what is behind it. Won't you try to think?'

She lay inert, eyes closed, hands lax in her lap. Her head rolled slowly. 'I don't know,' she said in a small, tired voice. 'I can't think. I don't want to try. All I want is to get away, to go somewhere where I can sleep. I'll go to a hotel, or somewhere, and after I've had some rest — ' Her voice dwindled.

They reached the bus station and Christopher could not decide if he should go in or not. He supposed she would expect him to wait with her. There were a number of people in the waiting room and he was glad; while he did not want to face them, he knew that the presence of people meant they had not had the bad luck of just missing the bus.

She was making no move to get out, and it suited him. 'Do you have any money?' he asked. Already he felt a little better.

She stirred and opened her eyes. 'Some. Enough, I hope.'

He pulled out his wallet and examined the contents. It contained two tens, a five and some ones. He removed all but two dollars. 'Here, take this. It isn't much, but it's all I have at the moment — take it! You'll need it if you're going to a hotel.'

Hesitantly she accepted the money. 'This makes me a whore, doesn't it,' she said in a listless voice.

He flushed. 'Damn it, Ruth. You can say some rather inept things yourself when you've a mind to.'

'I'm sorry. I really don't want to quarrel. I — thank you, Chris. I'm not very practical, I guess. There's something you could do for me, if you would.'

'Do?' He was nettled. 'Such as?'

'My things at the cottage. I'm not going back there ever, not if I can help it. All I have is some clothing and a few pictures and things. You'll be able to recognize them. Would you mind packing them in my trunk — it's in the closet — and having the trunk sent to my apartment? I hate to ask you, but I can't afford just to let them go.'

He reached over and clumsily touched her hand. 'Of course I'll do it. First thing in the morning. Are you sure that's all?'

She nodded slowly but did not speak. After a moment she withdrew her hand from the cover of his and rested it in her lap. From then on, for a half hour until the bus arrived, no word passed between them.

He saw her to the door. He handed up the overnight case and bade her a perfunctory goodbye. There was a little crush about the driver, and Ruth turned impulsively, threw her arms about Christopher's neck and kissed him.

He was too surprised to avoid it. Hastily he backed away.

★   ★   ★

He was striding to his car, hoping no one whom he knew had been in sight. He had passed the waiting room door when he heard his name called. He was dismayed; he did not know what to do, but he continued walking.

'Oh, Mr. Elliot!'

A man's voice. He did not at once recognize it but he could no longer ignore it. Defensively he turned and saw bearing down upon him one of the local policemen, a man by the name of Skaggs, whom he knew by sight.

'Oh, hello, Skaggs!' He forced himself to be jovial. 'Didn't hear you at first. What's wrong? Don't tell me I'm illegally parked.'

Skaggs came up. His small shrewd eyes swept beyond Christopher to inspect the car. 'Got kind of a bad scrape on that left side, Mr. Elliot,' he said. 'But there's nothin' wrong with your parkin'.'

The policeman came closer and after glancing about dropped his voice to a confidential level. 'Mr. Elliot, I know you're a friend of this here Mr. Donath's, and he's in the bus station there in pretty bad shape. He's tried to get on a couple different buses but the drivers wouldn't let him. Then he was raisin' hell in the bus station so they called me down here. Now, I don't want to put him in jail. He's a good fellow and everybody knows about what troubles he's been havin'. He's asleep now and he won't give no trouble. I thought maybe you wouldn't mind takin' him home, see?'

Skaggs stepped back, nodded his head crisply and closed his right eye in a knowing wink.

Christopher exhaled. 'Bill Donath? Of course I wouldn't mind. And thanks, Skaggs, for not running him in. Bill's not the worst fellow in the world.'

The policeman touched his cap. 'We catch a lot of hell sometimes, Mr. Elliot, but we ain't the worst people in the world either.'

★   ★   ★

The wheel of chance, around it goes, and where it stops, nobody knows.

Christopher, as Officer Skaggs helped him deposit Bill Donath's sagging form in the seat, could not but be reminded that

74

he had finally come, by whatever route, to fulfil his evening's mission. Because he was elated at the unexpected turn of affairs, he thanked Skaggs with a warmth that left the officer slightly nonplussed.

Mr. Skaggs couldn't see any occasion for happiness in taking home a stewed-up bum, even if he did happen to be a gentleman.

But Christopher was pleased. He considered the idea of taking Bill home; the presence of this unshaven, dirty and evil-smelling mess ought to convince Henrietta by allaying whatever suspicions she might have formed from the telephone call. And then, reluctantly, he decided against it.

He had trouble enough now without turning the place into a haven for dipsomaniacs.

Although Bill Donath's hair was thinning fast and he was developing a stomach, he was four or five years younger than Christopher. Under ordinary circumstances he dressed well and presented a favourable appearance. He had nice eyes and a quick smile and a way of making people feel that they had known him for a long time. With many of his clients that was as far as it progressed; close friends like Christopher, although they liked him, could not help but feel that he had a screw loose somewhere.

At the moment his friendship was a distinct liability. He had been drinking for days. Some time, or possibly several times during the course of it he had been quite evidently ill. At one point he must have been violently ejected from somewhere for his coat was torn, several buttons were missing and others hung by threads. His shoe tips had been scuffed through to their cloth linings.

Christopher's disgust was not unmixed with pity. A woman had caused this; who she was only Bill Donath knew, but anyone who cared could see her handiwork. How long could he keep it up? Economically, probably for a long time. Old Theodore had left him well fixed, and besides, his real estate and insurance business was one of those fool-proof affairs that run themselves. But physically

— Christopher glanced at the pinched, pasty skin with its tracery of purple veins; he listened to the faint, irregular breathing and he shook his head.

The Donath house, a rambling Colonial, was three blocks removed from his own and Christopher knew every inch of it, for it was a Donath and Elliot design. A light was burning in the living room and he thought it strange because he knew Bill lived alone, had no servant now, and probably hadn't been home for days.

The stopping of the car roused Bill, but he seemed to prefer the warmth and security of the front seat to the chill and uncertainty of the night. It was not until Christopher took him firmly by the belt and pulled a limp arm over his shoulder that Bill sighed and attempted to co-operate.

They were on the steps and Christopher was reaching for the door handle when the door opened and he came face to face with his brother-in-law, Wick.

* * *

Wick had been reading; the book was in his hand and a finger marked the place. Unhurriedly Wick stepped back, pulled off his glasses and placed the book carefully on the telephone stand. Then he removed and folded his glasses. Producing a case from his pocket he stowed the glasses in it and put the case away. His movements were as measured and deliberate as if he had been trying for a part in a play and this was a scene he had been given to do.

'Where did you find him?' Wick asked. His voice was as matter-of-fact as if it were four in the afternoon instead of four in the morning.

'At the bus station,' Christopher answered, swallowing surprise. 'Help me, will you? I don't believe I can manage him on the stairs.'

'Of course.'

Wick was neither as large nor as strong as Christopher. He was almost completely myopic and as he came in range he blinked owlishly in disapproval. 'Gad, he's filthy. Ugh! How would you suggest we manage?'

78

That was Wick. He couldn't say anything so simple as, 'What do you want me to do?' Christopher shrugged off annoyance. 'Take his feet and lead the way. I'll manage the rest of him.'

They had quite a time on the stairs. Bill came suddenly to life, objected strenuously, and his struggles nearly upset them. But Wick, at his end, was surprisingly firm and after several futile jerks Bill gave up.

They undressed him and Christopher was all for putting him under the shower, but Wick wouldn't hear of it. There would be time enough for that after he had slept, Wick said. Sleep was the only thing that could help repair the damage now.

Christopher didn't argue. He was alarmed by the rapid beat of Bill's heart. 'We'll have to find someone who can stay with him,' he said. 'We can't leave him alone. He'll have the rams when he comes out of it.'

'I'll stay,' Wick answered in a mild voice. 'I can make arrangements for Ashton to spell me at the Museum.' He was wearing his glasses again and he gave

Christopher a solicitous glance. 'That's a nasty cut you have there. You'd better wash it and use an antiseptic. I noticed iodine and tape in the medicine closet.'

Christopher lifted his hand and inspected it with annoyance. He had forgotten, for it gave him no pain. Then he noticed that there were still some slivers of glass on his coat sleeve.

He washed methodically and spilled iodine on the cut. While he was taping the hand he avoided looking at himself in the mirror. Helpful though Wick had been, he was annoyed at his presence; the inference was obvious. Had Henrietta used this direct and unsubtle method of checking on him, or had she been worried because he did not return and thinking he might need help, summoned from the only quarter she knew?

★ ★ ★

After three nightmarish hours in bed, Christopher arose a little before nine. His brain was pounding so it threatened to burst his skull. He could not bring himself to believe in the incredible happenings of the night, yet the ugly gash in his hand, a dull ache in his elbow, and the condition of his car were all salient reminders.

Force of habit directed him to the station parking plaza and there the sight of a uniformed policeman recalled to him his promise, and so he turned and headed for Echo Road.

The day was crisply bright, and his lack of sleep brought intensity and distortion of detail to familiar objects. Before he had reached the bridge he was suffering a severe headache; his eyes hurt so that he was forced to close his lids at intervals to keep the road from crowding in and crushing him. He had meant to see what damage he had done to the fence, but it was past him too quickly.

In the cottage driveway he found Ruth's second slipper; the other he retrieved from behind the hedge and he carried both into the house. As he stood in the living room the half-formed idea of finishing the previous night's search died within him. The place oppressed him. He could feel Ruth very strongly here. It would not have surprised him to see her come in from the kitchen and invite him to remove his coat and stay awhile.

The bottle of scotch remained where he had left it on the floor by the divan, and picking it up he drained the last of it. There had been more in the bottle than he realized. The liquor burned his mouth and throat and made his eyes water, but after it was down and had begun to spread, he felt considerably better.

He located the trunk, a half-sized wardrobe, in the hall closet and dragged it to the bedroom. He dumped in clothing and pictures without discrimination. He cleaned out the medicine cabinet and wrapped the contents in a bath towel, and this, together with shoes and toilet articles, he piled in with the rest.

Satisfied he had finished in the bedroom and bath he progressed to the kitchen where he could find nothing he thought might belong to her. He frowned at the mess and the broken outside door. Locating a broom he swept up glass fragments and deposited them in a waste-basket. Then he returned to the living room and there stood, glancing about in final inspection.

He was within a foot of the telephone when it rang.

As is frequently the case with people who carry considerable responsibility and are called upon to render many decisions, Christopher had relinquished certain of his more common or habitual actions to automatic control. Before he realized what he was doing he had picked up the telephone and had said, 'Hello?'

He received no answer.

He knew that the line was connected because the humming sound of the dial tone was absent. His gorge rose and he was about to speak angrily when belated caution held him. Suddenly rigid and wary he stood, trying to guess, to project his mind to the unseen other end and fathom the game.

Thus he waited for a full minute.

On the telephone or anywhere, sixty seconds of strained silence is apt to be unnerving and at the end of it he was sweating freely. But he heard no sound until at last a gentle *click* and then a droning buzz told him that the caller had hung up.

The incomprehensible business of the mouse forcibly returned to him. He stood shaking, glaring at the telephone as if it were an animate thing and he would destroy it. And then logic urged him to be calm. The caller had been expecting Ruth to answer, and not hearing her voice had been puzzled, had thought things over and had hung up.

Thus he reassured himself, but he was far from steadiness. He made a bungling job of closing the trunk. He fumbled so with the hasp that he reopened the cut in his hand.

It is a noteworthy fact that the Goddess of Ill Fortune does not always wait until we are prepared before she attacks us. Christopher had dragged the trunk to the tiny foyer and was in the act of opening the front door, when he saw a sedan on Echo Road. The sedan was proceeding slowly and the driver, its sole occupant, was eyeing the cottage.

It was Arthur Brokaw.

Christopher held himself rigid, hoping against hope that he was unrecognized. And then his heart nearly stopped when he remembered his car, parked in the drive. Arthur would hardly fail to spot it.

His worst fears were realized. In the road the sedan stopped and a door clunked solidly. Footsteps crunched in the gravel of the drive, came part way up the path and hesitated.

Christopher stood as if stricken, unable to think or move, hardly able to breathe. He could not see Arthur now; the crack of the door had closed against his weight. But he could hear him, shuffling hesitantly out there; now he was retracing toward the driveway, now stopping, now turning again.

For no reason, Cissie Folwell's indictment flashed through his brain: *Arthur Brokaw, of all the senseless and disconnected things you do, your bridge playing is the worst!*

Footsteps hurried up the path, the door opened and Arthur crowded into the tiny foyer.

Arthur, his small but bulbous form resplendent in loudly checked tweeds, acted as if he bore the cares of the world on his sloping shoulders. ''Lo, Chris,' he said in a breathless voice without looking up. 'Are the people home?'

Christopher, finding his tongue with difficulty, grunted, 'No.'

Arthur hurried a little way into the living room and looked wildly about. 'Cops said they found a broken door,' Arthur related hurriedly. 'Said they thought it might be a robbery. Thought I'd better check it.'

Christopher moved a step, shielding the trunk. He'd forgotten, if he'd ever known, that Arthur owned the cottage. 'No, it wasn't a robbery,' his voice came reluctantly. 'It was an accident.'

'Oh!' Arthur appeared to be tremendously relieved.

'Oh, I'm glad. That's fine — ' He hesitated, tried to bring his eyes to meet Christopher's and failed. 'Coming to your office soon. Big job for you — see you later.'

As hastily as he had come, and

apparently as senselessly, Arthur Brokaw departed.

When the sedan had moved away, Christopher dragged the trunk to the flagstone steps and left it there. He returned swiftly to the telephone, called the first drayman who came to his mind, gave the location of the trunk and the address to which it should be delivered, and then fled.

His obligation to Ruth, so far as he was concerned, was ended.

★   ★   ★

It was after noon when Christopher arrived at his office. He had stopped en route for lunch, and the presence of food within him lent him a false freshness. He was grateful to find Margaret out; he was in no mood to be bossed by anyone.

There was much to do and he plunged into it. He worked at top speed, for it was the only way he knew. He had never stopped to reason why, but something within him drove him to go faster and faster. He was not a perfectionist. He abhorred the waste of time that perfection demanded, but he did aim for an approach as near to it as speed would permit.

He liked to think that no matter what line of endeavour he might try he would be successful, and in this he was likely right, or very nearly so.

Christopher had been working for an hour; the problems of Ruth and the white cottage had faded to the background and he was beginning to feel himself again when Arthur Brokaw and Lambie Pie arrived.

''Lo. Hard at it, I see,' Arthur wheezed.

He jumped up. He was completely nonplussed. The focus of his mind returned with sickening clarity to the scene in the white cottage. Even if he could think of anything to say, he could not speak. He even forgot to offer them chairs.

But Arthur was not one to miss an opportunity for gallantry, and bustling like a rooster he found a chair for Lambie Pie and another for himself. In the presence of his 'creatures', Arthur always seemed to glow. Why he had so much trouble keeping them was a mystery to all save the creatures themselves.

Arthur raised his head until something like a chin was evident. 'Remember I mentioned a big job?' he asked breathlessly. 'Well, here it is. Take a look at these. Fourteen in all. Want to do the whole lot. Complete.'

Christopher accepted the photographs Arthur handed him and sat down heavily. Automatically his eyes sought the glossy prints and mechanically he shuffled through them. 'Fourteen,' he finally responded. His voice was weak.

'Thought it would knock you.' Arthur grinned happily. He turned to his wife. 'Didn't I tell you it would knock him, Lambie Pie?'

'Ya-as, Arthur.' She covered a yawn.

'Eighty thousand,' Arthur said carefully. His grin continued but his eyes were less happily vague. 'That's the limit. Spread it out so's it will do the most good. You know the neighbourhoods; spend the most in the best neighbourhoods. There are houses in there worth anywhere from four to forty thousand; use your own judgment. I've put on the back of each snapshot what they seem to need the most. Couple need new heating plants, some need plumbing. I'll turn it all over to you, but the outside limit on any house is twenty-five per cent of the value and hold the lot down to eighty thousand.' He paused anxiously. 'Naturally, I expect to pay you more than the usual fee for this kind of work, but keep it down. If it pays off I'll do the rest of my houses.'

'Don't forget,' Lambie Pie yawned, 'to tell him about the kitchens.'

'Oh, yes. Kitchens.' Arthur glowed. 'Spend plenty on kitchens. It's the woman who rents the house. That's my wife's idea.' He glanced fondly at her, and when she had finished her current yawn she favoured him with a vague smile. 'And you'd better work with Bill Donath's office; he's my agent. Don't want people to start moving out just because — '

Lambie Pie let out a shriek.

Christopher jerked about violently, and Arthur was so startled he dropped the photograph.

90

'My bag! I left it in the restaurant! It's got my diamond wristwatch in it!'

Arthur stared vapidly. 'Your bag,' he repeated.

Lambie Pie was halfway across the outer office before Arthur had collected his wits sufficiently to follow her.

*   *   *

Christopher had expected that Ruth would call him; as he remembered, that was the way it had been left. She was going to a hotel, she said, to get some rest; when she'd had time to think, she would get in touch with him. He did not want to become further involved with her, but he did feel that he was due an explanation of some sort. He was becoming increasingly worried about last night's affair; worried and uneasy because he did not know just how far its causes might affect him.

When at five o'clock he had received no word, he was as annoyed with her for not calling as he had previously been because she had.

The Brokaws' explosive visit had ruined the afternoon for him. That and Margaret's return. He had lost his stride. Over and over he shuffled the photographs, read the notes on the back, made meaningless notes of his own and in the end invariably returned to the glossy print of the cottage on Echo Road.

Arthur owned the cottage and the rental was handled by Bill Donath. It was at Bill's house that he had met Ruth. Ruth Cassell and Bill Donath.

At his elbow the telephone set up a jangling disturbance.

'Hello — Donath and Elliot.' He had almost forgotten that the rest of them had gone home.

'Mr. Elliot, please. Mr. Christopher Elliot.'

'Speaking.'

A gurgling chuckle. 'Mis-ter Elliot,' the man's voice repeated in insulting parody.

'That's right.' Christopher's gorge rose. 'What do you want?'

'He asks me, what do I want?' The caller chuckled again.

'See here, I'm busy. State your business

if you have any, otherwise you'll oblige me by hanging up.'

'All right, Mister Elliot.' The voice continued to be insultingly amused, but an edge of sharpness crept into it. 'I'm a businessman myself. You don't know me, Mister Elliot, and I'm not going to introduce myself because we aren't going to mention any names. I'll state my business, simple and plain. I'm being paid by a certain party to keep tabs on you and another party — we don't need to mention any names, do we, Mister Elliot?'

Christopher's mouth went dry. He could not make his tongue behave. He tried to prime his mouth and his lips with his tongue; the action was less effective than pushing a cocoa mat across sandpaper. 'I don't know what you're talking about,' he managed to get out.

'Oh, I think you do all right. You know and I know and a certain other party is going to know if you and I don't get together. Or maybe you think I'm only bluffing, Mister Elliot. Shall I tell you where she lives and where she works and what she does; what she wears and how she likes to kick off her shoes when she gets home at night? I guess we don't need to mention names, do we, Mister Elliot?'

So you're the one who has been following her, Christopher thought. 'What do you want?'

'That's better, Mister Elliot. A lot better. I thought we might get together somewhere and have a little chat. I'm a businessman and I figured that if my time is worth something to this first party I spoke about, then maybe it might be worth something to you. That's logical, isn't it, Chris? You don't mind if I call you Chris, do you?'

Cat and mouse. Contemptible swine. 'You go to hell,' Christopher said hoarsely.

'Oh, a tough guy, eh? Well, put this down. I'm giving you time to think things over. I'll give you until, say, tomorrow night at this same time. Is that too soon? Make it the day after tomorrow then. You'd better write this down: Call Grant two, six-seven-seven-oh. Got that? Grant two, six-seven-seven-oh. Just leave a message for Mr. Axelrod to call Doctor Ruth. That's all.'

The line went blank, and then the dial hum came on.

Christopher sat almost completely numb. So this was how it worked. The unseen was employed by someone to watch you, but the unseen was unscrupulous. He thought you might be made to pay more than the someone, and his services were on the auction block.

The beginnings of blackmail.

Suddenly cool, he inserted the eraser of his pencil into the dial and clicked off the numbers. He sat back composedly and listened to the ringing. A woman's voice responded by simply repeating the numbers.

'Good afternoon. To whom am I speaking, please?'

'This is the Central Office Service. We answer your telephone at any time of day or night. Our fees are moderate. Did you wish to subscribe to our service?'

'Not at the moment. Do you have a Mr. Axelrod listed?'

'Axelrod? Hold the line, please . . . No,

we have no one by that name. However, he might be connected with one of the companies we serve. Would you care to leave a message?'

'No, thank you. It's not important.'

Christopher sat back and thoughtfully eyed the telephone. Axelrod. That wasn't his name, naturally. He wouldn't let himself be traced so easily. But what if the whole thing was a frame-up: if, instead of hounding Ruth, he was actually working with her?

He dialled Ruth's number and, after a long wait, hung up. He had begun to smile grimly; on a hunch he asked Information for the listing of Ruth's apartment house, and presently he was given the janitor.

'Miss Cassell, in 3C? Sorry, I'm not supposed to give out that information. Who's calling?'

'Sergeant Murphy, police department,' Christopher answered savagely.

'Oh, yes sir, Sergeant. I'm glad she took my advice, about the man who was following her, I mean. I told her to go to you. I tried to catch him, and I've been keeping watch — is Miss Cassell all right?'

'That's one of the things I'm trying to find out, you idiot!'

'Oh, yes sir, Sergeant. I'm sorry. You know, sometimes cranks call up. No sir, she hasn't been here for a couple of days, and she isn't back yet because I was just up there with the evening paper and nobody was in. Is there anything I can do, Sergeant?'

'No,' Christopher said.

He pushed away from his desk and glanced at his watch. Six o'clock. Still plenty of time to make the six-ten. As he stood up he glanced from the window into the areaway and he saw, on the fifth floor in the rear, the light of another late worker. A thought seized him: perhaps the unknown was a tenant of this building. He might even now be in one of those dark windows, watching and chuckling. He might have been sitting in the security of nearness, observing Christopher's every move while he telephoned.

Christopher wasn't so sure of himself,

now. When he left the building, instead of walking to the station as he usually did, he hailed a cab.

4

One ray of sun found its way through the swiftly gathering clouds.

When Christopher reached home he found a surprise waiting for him. Teena, bundled in a quilted robe, had come downstairs and was expectantly standing in the hall.

He had always prided himself upon being unemotional but now quick tears welled to his eyes. He dropped to his knees and gathered her in his arms.

Only this mattered, nothing more.

Teena was passive at first. Then she began to wriggle. 'Let me go, Daddy. You're spoiling it.'

He did not want to let her go, but when her struggles increased he reluctantly allowed her to quit the haven of his arms. Standing, he backed away, and she remained with tiny fists clenched, arms thrust straight down, her small round face set in the utmost concentration.

'When I was sick and lay abed,' Teena recited, 'I had two pillows at my head — ' She paused. Her eyes clouded and then swiftly cleared. 'And all my toys beside me lay — and all my toys beside me lay — ' She looked beseechingly up the stairs. 'Mommy!'

Henrietta's quiet voice prompted, 'To keep me — '

'To keep me happy all the day. God bless Mommy an' Daddy an' Wickie an' make me a good girl. A-men!' She finished in a rush.

Henrietta came down the stairs. Her eyes held pride and she said, 'We rehearsed that all afternoon, just for you, Daddy. Doctor Slade said it would be all right for us to get up and surprise you. And we have another surprise, too — '

The 'other surprise' could contain himself no longer. Wickie came clattering breathlessly down the stairs. 'I'm home, Daddy, and gee, is it good! Did you bring the evening paper? Mommy's going to read us the funnies. I haven't had the funnies in a long time. Granny doesn't get the same paper we do.'

Christopher lifted Teena into his arms. He pulled Wickie to him and held the curly head against his stomach. His eyes sought Henrietta, and in answer to his appeal she moved closer and impulsively put her arm about him.

Only this was real.

'Daddy, the *funnies*!'

'Yes, Daddy,' Henrietta sighed and drew away. 'And there are other things. Wick and Lyman will be here for dinner. They're due at almost any moment. I'm afraid you'll have to hurry.'

The happiness drained from him. He put Teena down and, without the customary scuffle, gave Wickie the newspaper.

'I'm sorry to be late,' he said. 'Arthur Brokaw brought in a stack of work. He wants to remodel fourteen houses. I don't know just how we'll do for material. I suppose we should have cocktails before dinner.'

Henrietta made a fleeting search of his face. 'You must be awfully tired, Chris. I'd hoped you might get a chance to catch up on sleep during the day. You needn't

101

come down unless you want to. I can manage. I wouldn't have asked them, but Wick wants to talk to you about Bill, and I thought Lyman would be amusing.'

'I'll make it. Give me ten minutes for a shower and a drink, and I'll be good as new.'

★   ★   ★

'Bill Donath,' Wick recounted as he accepted a Martini and carefully moved nearer the fireplace mantel, 'has the most amazing resistance I've ever seen.' He paused, bent his head and glanced partly through and partly over his eyeglasses. 'Perhaps I should not say 'resistance,' although there must be resistance before there is recovery.'

Christopher was incredulous. 'Do you mean to say that he's all right?'

'I didn't say he was all right,' Wick blandly corrected him. 'He isn't. He's a very sick man indeed. But when he awoke at noon he was completely sober. Moreover, he didn't ask for whisky. He asked for water.'

Ashton lowered his drink. A muscle in his homely face twitched. 'Remarkable. You gave it to him?'

'I gave him a small quantity,' Wick replied with dignity. 'I knew precisely what to do. I had spent considerable time during the course of the night in perusing von Runstedt's *Alcoholism: Causes and Treatment*. I also spent additional time in consulting Doctor Slade. Bill was extremely shaky, but fortunately he was suffering none of the usual hallucinations attendant upon protracted drinking. I managed to induce him to consume a quantity of soup, after which he went back to sleep and slept quite well until four o'clock this afternoon.'

'When he awoke at that time,' Wick frowned, 'the story was slightly different.'

Ashton leaned forward. 'Snakes, eh? Pink elephants and that sort of thing?'

'Oh, no. He wasn't delirious at any time. But when he awoke at four he was suffering violently from remorse. I have never seen a man in a lower mental state. He was completely unsparing of himself.'

Christopher felt a tightening of his

throat. 'I suppose he went into his domestic troubles.'

Wick nodded. 'I should say he did.'

'Did he happen to mention the name of the other woman?' Christopher hoped he sounded casual.

'The other woman?' Wick shot him a glance. 'I didn't inquire. I felt it was none of my business. When he's ready, I suppose, he'll tell us the whole story.' Wick sighed. 'Poor devil; he wanted to shave himself, but I didn't dare trust him with a razor. You know, a man in his condition — ' He made a suggestive movement with his hand across his throat.

'You didn't leave him there alone, did you?' Lyman Ashton demanded.

'Naturally not.' Wick's glance was withering. 'I had Slade send a nurse around. Bill took a sedative, and when I left he was sleeping like a child.'

Christopher was both angered and dissatisfied with Wick's answer to his question. Despite the rebuff he would have pursued the subject further, had not Henrietta arrived to announce dinner and subsequently deprived him of the opportunity.

As they moved toward the dining room Ashton dropped back and linked his arm through Christopher's. 'Would you have in your library,' he asked, 'any books about old houses? I'm doing an antebellum yarn and I'm stuck for background material. I've combed the Folwell; Wick lets me run around there pretty much as I please. But confidentially,' he lowered his voice, 'they have the mustiest collection of trash you ever saw.'

Christopher nodded. 'I have any number of them. After dinner you're welcome to go in and help yourself.' He caught Ashton's speculative glance at Wick, and it occurred to him that the writer might also be pondering the biological miracle that had made it possible to spawn two such totally different persons as Wick and Henrietta from the same roe.

★ ★ ★

He had not meant to stay up late. He was dead for sleep, and nerves and flesh cried for bed. But there had been highballs after dinner; Ashton, changeable as a chameleon, had come up with a reminiscent mood, and in the afterglow time had simply disappeared.

A hard fellow to make out, Ashton. He had been everywhere, and as he freely admitted, had travelled every class. When he chose, he could be entertaining as the devil. He knew an amazing number of people and had an apparently endless supply of anecdotes; he knew just how far to go and he stopped well on the safe side of boredom.

If he had ever been married, he made no mention of it. He talked freely and impersonally of himself, yet revealed surprisingly little. There seemed to be no conceit in him, but he was unquestionably self-centred. He made it evident that he would be ruthless if his habits or personal pleasures were interfered with. Because he was a writer, Christopher put him down as eccentric and thus despatched him.

It was past eleven when Ashton departed with the books, and Christopher could not have slept had he desired.

He sat in his study; Henrietta had long ago gone to bed. He sat, staring at nothing and thinking nothing, yet seeing a great many things. Fleeting pictures so disturbing he kept jumping from one to another. He was certainly not drunk; he knew his capacity and he knew how much he had had. He did not want to drink. He had an instinctive feeling that under the pressure on him now, if he started he would be unable to stop. He was sober, but he felt the detachment of mind — the paradoxical ability to solve all problems and inability to face any — so frequently felt by the drinker.

It was on Ruth, principally, that the thought pictures centred. He knew it was bad to keep her in his mind; he did not fear it would destroy him, but surely it would do him no good. He was through with her, yet he could not let her go. He recalled the memory of her last kiss. It had startled and annoyed him then, but now he remembered it only as an idyll of sweet surrender.

She had told him how she loathed and

despised him. She told him too she thought him responsible for all that had terrified her. Yet after a single kindly word, one friendly gesture, she had thrust all else aside. Had thrown her hurt arms about his neck and put her bruised mouth to his. I am yours, she had said in effect; take me, do with me what you will.

Christopher thought of the dark bruises on her creamy skin, and suddenly he wanted her.

He arose restlessly, pacing from wall to wall of his study, fighting his want, trying to drive her out. It was no good. He could not go on like this. He would go smash. The wreckage would make Bill Donath seem a sainted lily in comparison. But he wanted her. He wanted now to put on his coat and hat, or hatless and coatless drive to the city in search of her. To roam the streets, watching for her face and listening for the sound of her voice.

He hated her. Under this roof with him were all he held most dear. A tiny girl of four, memorizing a verse just to please him. A boy who would one day grow to be his image and likeness. A woman who had trusted in him and shared with him and given to him, and would continue to trust, share and give so long as he earned her love and respect.

The memory of Ruth's bleeding feet.

He could not banish her from his mind, could not erase the hurts of her flesh, the bruises of her face, her mutilated hands. Why was it not pity he felt, but desire? What was he? What had happened to him?

He was near exhaustion when a burring, familiar ringing sound shattered the stillness of the house.

His pacing stopped and he whirled about. In heaven's name, who at this hour? Angrily he strode to the hall and grasped the telephone.

He hated it, this inanimate thing for him associated with everything undesirable.

'Who is it?' he asked roughly.

For a moment there was silence. And then he shivered violently and the hackles reared on his neck as a sound came over the wire.

The lonely, tortured meowing of a cat.

New sounds awakened in the house. Upstairs a door opened. There was a plaintive cry, the soft pad of feet along the bare upper hallway. But he stood rooted at the telephone, the receiver frozen to his ear.

And then, abruptly, it was over, and there was no sound save sanity. The recognizable, persistent and humdrum buzzing of the dial.

Teena came padding down the stairs. She circled the newel post and came up to him. She was crying softly and her outstretched hands tenderly carried an object half-concealed.

'Look, Daddy,' the child sobbed. 'See what I found. A little white Mickey Mouse, all cold.'

$\star$ $\star$ $\star$

He was hardly sane, and when he understood what it was she had said and what she carried, he went off his head completely.

He made a lunging, sweeping grab, shouted, 'Give me that!' and snatched the horrible thing from her hands. Then he towered above her. His eyes protruded from his livid face. His lips were savagely distorted and the cords of his neck were swollen.

'Where did you get this?'

The child stood rigid, too frightened to run or speak.

'Answer me, damn you!' He advanced threateningly.

'*Where did you get this?*'

The child was immobile and unanswering, numb with fascination.

'You — '

'*Chris!*'

A terrified cry, a rush on the stairs, and Henrietta's face intervened.

'You keep out of this! Teena, answer me!'

Henrietta's arms and body gave protection to the child.

She faced him with blazing eyes. 'Have you gone mad?' she cried. 'What are you doing to her? What do you mean, shouting at her? You know how ill she has been. Chris, answer me, are you out of your mind?'

He could not answer. He could scarcely hear. The furies so suddenly released within him scurried for freedom, and the door from which they had escaped hung useless and idle. Emptiness sifted from the cell it had guarded and slowly filled his brain.

'*Teena, darling, it's Mommy. Everything's all right. It was just a bad dream —* '

The poison of violence seeped from him slowly. One after another the cells of sanity awoke, bestirred themselves, and took command.

'*You're awake now. Mommy's here. Everything is all right, darling, everything is all right —* '

The child quivered, went limp and broke into convulsive sobbing.

Henrietta lifted her and began slowly to ascend the stairs.

The closing of a door was the spark that roused Christopher from his stupor. Shakily he raised his hand, intending to brush it across his forehead and then he realized that the hand still held the dead mouse. In sudden anger he flung the thing the length of the hall and stood glaring. And then, as suddenly, he was after it; running headlong, stopping to search in the dark corner beyond his open study door.

The mouse eluded him and he dropped to his knees. He was panting in frantic haste. His eyes became more accustomed to the gloom, and then he found it. Clutching the thing triumphantly he carried it to his study. He put it on his desk, sat in his chair and in the sterile light of the fluorescent lamp, studied it.

A mouse. A white mouse. Dead.

He inhaled a sharply deep and uneven breath. This was no illusion, no trick of an overtaxed brain. He was sitting here at his desk. He could see familiar objects about him: the fireplace, the mantel clock, the books and pictures. He could hear familiar sounds: water being drawn in the bathroom, hurried footsteps in the upper hall, Wickie's voice saying 'What was it, Mommy? What was it?' The clunk of a closing door.

He forced himself to look away from

the mouse and began pulling out drawers. He found a box that held paper clips and dumped the clips in a pile, but the box was too small. He found another box, one that had contained erasers, but it was too shallow.

His search had turned to furious rummaging when he heard Henrietta's footsteps on the stairs.

In quick desperation he seized an envelope, stuffed the mouse inside it and hid the envelope in his pocket. He swept objects indiscriminately into drawers and was rearranging his desk when Henrietta came in.

She looked years older and more tired, but she had no tears. She eyed him levelly, holding herself with deadly calm. She came directly to the desk and stood without speaking.

He could not face her. 'I can imagine,' he sighed, 'how it must have looked and sounded to you. I guess I lost my head. I had fallen asleep and was having a frightful nightmare when the telephone woke me. I was still half in the dream when I went out in the hall and found

Teena. She startled me so I shouted at her — '

'Chris, I've had enough.'

'I can't blame you. I'm dreadfully sorry, Henrietta, I just wasn't myself — '

'I'm leaving you, Chris.'

'I know it sounds — ' He caught his breath. Quick terror came into his eyes. 'You — what did you say?'

'I'm leaving you, Chris. For good. I'd go now but Mother isn't well and I don't want to upset her at this hour. I'll wait until morning. You may make whatever arrangements you like about the house. Agnes will go with me.'

'You — no!' He jumped from the chair, knocking it over in his haste. He was around the desk and he grasped her in his arms. 'In God's name, you don't mean that. I know how it looks, but you've got to stand by me. You can't just walk out on me now!'

She was ice in his arms. 'I don't want to talk about it, Chris.'

'You don't know what you are saying. Whatever I may have done, or you fancy I've done, you can't leave me when I'm in trouble.' He began to tremble. 'You wouldn't do that to a dog. You must give me a little time. You've got to see me through. You can't go now; you couldn't be so cruel.'

'Is that all you have to say?'

He was stunned. His eyes searched her, seeking desperately for some sign. He said, more slowly, 'I must find out who or what it is, this thing I'm fighting, before I can explain anything to you. I ask only that you give me a little time, perhaps one or two days. If at the end of it you still want to leave me I'll not stand in your way. But to go now, without giving me a chance — you can't do it, Henrietta. You can't.'

'Are you finished?'

This woman whom he knew, with whom he had lived and loved and laughed, and sometimes fought; who had dwelt with him in light and darkness, whose every mood and movement, thought, dislike, desire, hope, habit, motive, ambition, taste, fear, were all known to him — this woman he did not know at all.

116

It was because of his affair with Ruth. He had meant to tell her, to confess and ask forgiveness, but now it was too late. She knew; she had known all along.

His arms dropped down slowly. The last vestige of colour departed his face.

'It won't be necessary for you to go,' he said stiffly. 'This is your home: yours and Teena's and Wickie's. I'll pack a few things. I'll leave as soon as I've finished some work in here.'

She was not listening to him.

★ ★ ★

He was not quite sane. Familiar things had somehow suddenly become unfamiliar to him. The empty bedroom was strange, distorted and out of proportion. The beds, one rumpled with covers thrown full back and the other with sheet and blanket folded part way down, were completely foreign things.

He went to the tallboy and quietly pulled out drawers. He gathered gloves, linen, neckwear, shirts, socks, a small pistol, a belt, a box of buttons and studs, and with unaccustomed care laid them in his Gladstone. His movements were precise but without plan; he seemed not to know what he was doing. A jade-framed picture of Henrietta stood on the tallboy. He took the picture down, inspected it gravely and then carefully removed the photograph from the frame. The photograph he smoothed beneath a flap in his bag and returned the frame to its place on the tallboy.

His glance wandered about the bed-room as if trying to comprehend its new proportions. His eyes were dead, fumbling with strangeness. His gaze wavered, fell on his bed, jumped, wavered momentarily and then sharply returned.

Sanity found him with shocking impact.

His bed. After it was made up, during day and evening and until the moment for his occupancy, the bed was covered with a candlewick spread from foot to top. But now the spread had been carefully folded down until it covered only the lower quarter of the bed. Sheet and blanket also were folded, part way, on a bias.

Inhaling quickly he moved to the head of the bed. Only the pillow and the upper half of the bed were mussed.

He straightened and his eyes narrowed. Teena had been sleeping here. Henrietta had granted her this special favour, permitting her to remain until he came upstairs. She had been in his bed when the sound of the telephone had roused her.

The mouse, then, had been on his pillow; either on or under it.

He was thoughtful as he closed his Gladstone bag and quietly crossed the room. When he reached the light switch he stood hesitant with his hand on it, glancing across the hall to the door of the guest bedroom where Henrietta had chosen to go.

And then, exhaling slowly, he switched off the light and, noiselessly crossing to the landing, went down the stairs.

★　★　★

Grey dawn was edging in at the windows when Christopher initialled what he had written. It had not been easy to write. He folded the pages carefully and sealed them in an envelope. He wrote *Henrietta* across the face of it. The clock was striking six when he propped the envelope against the telephone and left the house.

★　★　★

A steam bath, a shave and food might be poor substitutes for sleep, but Christopher had time for nothing else. He registered at the City Club and asked the desk to telephone Lyman Ashton to have lunch with him there. He had no plan, but he knew now that he needed help and advice and Ashton, he felt, could be trusted.

He spent precious moments in a futile attempt to contact Ruth at her apartment; he tried a few hotels where she might be a guest, and gave it up.

Very likely she would be using an assumed name.

He pondered, too, the advisability of

employing a private detective and that too he gave up. Already a target for extortion, he had no desire to increase the difficulty of his position. In point of fact, he was greatly confused. He did not know what he should do, but of one thing he was certain: the time for waiting had passed.

The day was sultry and Christopher was sweating freely when he had covered the three blocks between the City Club and the Professional Building. He entered the lobby and sought the directory, but the names on it meant nothing to him and so he consulted the car-starter.

'Not just sure whom I want to see,' Christopher admitted. 'We — er — have an animal that died, and I'd like to find out if it was poisoned or what.'

'We got no vets here,' the attendant thought out loud. He was scowling in concentration. 'Let's see — maybe Swinburne. He's a patho-something or other. Tenth floor. You might try him.'

Christopher went up to the tenth floor.

He had not long to wait. The attractive receptionist who took his card returned almost immediately. At her nod he entered an inner office and faced a lean, leathery and completely bald little man.

'Mr. Elliot? You're the architect, aren't you? Ted Donath was a close friend of mine. Believe your firm designed this building. What can I do for you?'

Christopher took the envelope from his pocket. 'Maybe you'll think I'm nutty as a fruitcake, but I'd like to know what killed this mouse. And anything more about it you can tell me.'

The pathologist shrugged, pulled a sheet of paper from his drawer and emptied the contents of the envelope on it. A faint light of amusement flickered in his eyes and was gone.

'A white mouse, sometimes popular with the younger generation. Had a cage of 'em myself when I was a kid.' His quizzical eyes glanced up. 'Mind telling me the circumstances under which this died?'

'I don't know the circumstances. It was found dead.'

'Hm. No abrasions on the hide. Appears to be rather young, which might eliminate one of the natural causes. There is a certain amount of lividity apparent which would make me suspect gas. Mice as well as canaries, you know, are sometimes used by miners to detect the presence of gas in close tunnels. I'll perform a complete autopsy if you want, but it will take some time. What else do you want to know about it?'

'I don't know. Whatever there is.'

'I see.' The pathologist's restless eyes sharpened briefly. 'All right. We'll do what we can. You might be interested to know that we had a similar request; about a year ago I believe it was. I don't recall the exact circumstances, but I remember that they were peculiar. As I recall it, some woman was frightened almost out of her wits — what's wrong, Mr. Elliot? Are you ill?'

'Could you locate the woman's name in your files?'

'Hm, well, possibly. It would take some time since I don't recall the exact date. However, we can try if it's important.'

Christopher laughed harshly. 'It's important, all right. As soon as you find it, please call me at my office.'

$\star$ $\star$ $\star$

Lyman Ashton, a look of complete incredulity on his homely face, leaned forward in the deep leather chair. 'Impossible!' he ejaculated. 'It's the damnedest story I ever heard. You mean to tell me that the fellow Axelrod expects you to call him tomorrow night?'

'He does.'

'And all the business about the cat and mouse actually happened?'

'It did.'

Ashton searched his face anxiously. 'Impossible!' he repeated, but with less vehemence than before.

'It happened, Ashton, believe me,' Christopher said grimly. 'Not only did it happen but because of it, Henrietta has left me. I can't say as I blame her. I've been no one to live with for quite some time. When I saw the mouse in Teena's hands last night I completely lost my head. Henrietta will never forgive me for swearing at her.'

'Amazing.' Ashton shook his head. 'Absolutely incredible. I'm damned!'

Christopher sighed. 'Now I'm trying to locate Ruth. She was to call me as soon as she had caught up on rest, but she hasn't. I've simply got to get information from her: find out who it is she's been connected with or done something to, whoever might dislike her enough to do a thing of this sort. Or,' he breathed in slowly, 'find out if she's in on the shakedown.'

Ashton, it appeared, was following him with difficulty. The writer's face held a pinkish tinge and his eyes were slightly glazed. 'Do you mean,' he asked, 'that you know nothing about her? About her past life; whom she went with or might have been married to or where she came from?'

'Nothing.'

'Or — er — who might have been staying with her when you weren't?'

'Our relationship,' Christopher's cheeks reflected some of Ashton's pinkness, 'wasn't as involved as I may make it sound. We — well, I was indiscreet but I had no hold over her. It was just something that happened. She knew I was married; she asked no questions. It never occurred to me that I knew nothing whatever about her.' He spread his hands in a gesture of helplessness.

Ashton leaned back. 'You say you've tried to locate her?'

'I've done little more than telephone her apartment. I realize that's not very intelligent. I don't want to employ a detective. My experience with Mr. Axelrod has been quite enough. But I've got to find her. The idea may not sound sensible, but I'd like to know if it was she with whom Bill Donath was involved.'

'Donath? It doesn't make sense.'

'It was through Bill that I met her; it was Bill who found the house for her, the cottage on Echo Road.'

'But his affair and yours were almost coincidental. How could he have been seeing her without your knowledge?'

'I don't know. Naturally, I didn't spend all my time with her. She told me I didn't know anything about her or about other women.' Christopher grinned mirthlessly. 'What a balled-up mess!'

'Donath is coming along. Wick told me

he went to work this morning. If you wanted me to I could, er — ' Ashton paused hopefully.

'No. I want to learn from her.'

'Just what do you want me to do?'

'I'm not sure. Keep an eye on Henrietta and the children, perhaps. We might be dealing with a maniac. So long as the cat and mouse business affected only Ruth, I could feel sympathetic but not alarmed. Now that it has entered my home — ' His voice trailed and his eyes became grim and hard with introspection.

They were in a sheltered alcove that at other times was used for bridge and backgammon. In front of and some distance from them moved small groups of men, heading to or from the bar and grill rooms. In the near foreground a broad table was spread with magazines, and in a chair by it a white-haired member dozed with a newspaper crumpled in his lap.

It was all quite calm, sane and well-ordered.

Ashton glanced anxiously at Christopher. What he saw did not reassure him.

'In the beginning,' Ashton said, 'you told me you wanted my advice. I'll give it now. My advice is to stay away from this woman. Stay completely away from her. Make peace with Henrietta and tell Axelrod to go to hell, but stay away from the woman. You'll only get yourself in deeper water. In the meantime, I'll do what I can.'

Ashton arose, acting as if he expected Christopher to do likewise. When Christopher did not, he lingered a moment. 'Give it up, old man,' he said earnestly. 'Forget the wild-goose chase. Even if she telephones you, ignore her. Don't go near her. Getting your wife and children back is more important than anything the woman could possibly have to tell you. Believe me. I'm not as young as you are. I know.'

But his advice, he found, fell on deaf ears. Shrugging, he went out and when he reached the street he took a white linen handkerchief from his breast pocket.

Mopping face and forehead, Ashton said, 'Damn!' rather sharply and started in search of a cab.

★ ★ ★

'Wait here. I don't know just how long I'll be, but wait.' Christopher slid from cab seat to pavement and hurriedly inspected the front of the building. A fitful wind sent eddies of street dust and plane leaves across the pavement and into a declivity marked by a short flight of concrete steps. Hastily he crossed to the steps, ran down them and pressed a button beneath a neat brass *Deliveries* sign.

Presently the door opened and a man, neither young nor old, dressed in faded overalls and a sweater, asked him what he wanted.

'I'm trying to locate Miss Cassell. She lives in 3C in this building, but she has not answered her telephone for several days.'

The man in overalls shrugged. 'She hasn't been here for several days, mister.'

'She left for here, taking the bus, Sunday night. Or rather it was early Monday morning. She intended, she said, on stopping at a hotel, and she was to call me. Since she was in need of clothing I

129

thought she might have stopped here before going to the hotel. In any event she hasn't kept her promise to call me. Because of circumstances, I'm worried. I'd like to enter her apartment.'

The overalled man drew back. 'Oh, I couldn't let you do that. It's against all the rules. I'm not allowed to admit anyone unless they're a tenant, or else one of the tenants has spoken to me about it.'

'Not even in an emergency? Suppose something might have happened to her.'

'Oh, I don't think so.'

'In other words, you're not going to let me in?'

'That's right, mister.'

'Then I'll go to the police!'

'Okay.' The overalled one shrugged.

Christopher fought against unreasoning anger. 'What about the trunk that came for her? Who paid the charges on it? Who signed for it?'

'Trunk? What trunk?'

'The trunk that was delivered here either yesterday or the day before.'

'Trunk? There didn't any trunk come for her. I did get a trunk up out of the cellar for her about two weeks ago so's she could send it off someplace, but none's come here.'

'You — you're sure?'

'Positive certain, I'm sure. No trunk for Miss Cassell, no trunk for anybody. I guess I'd know.'

★   ★   ★

Landon, resplendent in frock coat and striped morning trousers, rushed forward with the easy grace that some fat men possess. 'Mr. Elliot! Glad to see you, sir. You haven't been here in a long time — come right in, sir. Come right in and sit down!'

'No.' Christopher glanced impatiently away and attempted to penetrate the heavy drapes separating showroom from workshop. 'I really haven't the time. We have a terrific remodelling job for Arthur Brokaw and I thought I might have Miss Cassell work with me on some of the details. Is she here?'

'No-o-o.' Landon's full lips formed a circle and his generous forehead

131

wrinkled in the faintest of frowns. 'Miss Cassell hasn't worked for the past two weeks. She seemed awfully distraught, poor thing, and I suggested she take a rest. She'd been working awfully hard, you know, and the work is rather trying. Some of the clients — ' Landon threw up his hands. 'Why don't you try Claryse Woolfolk? An awfully clever little girl. She's done some of the grandest things. You know the Baker house? That's her work, all of it. An awfully clever job. I'm sure you'd find Miss Woolfolk satisfactory in every respect.'

'I would prefer to see Ruth Cassell. We can talk about someone else later on. Has Ruth been in touch with you? Would you know how to reach her?'

'Really, Mr. Elliot.' Signs of annoyance appeared in Landon's chins. 'I have no idea where she might be. Have you tried her apartment?'

'I have. Could you tell me where she came from? That is, where her home is located?'

'Oh, I suppose we have it in the

records. You might ask the book-keeper — ' Landon's petulance changed instantly to beaming radiance. 'Ah, good morning Mrs. Sansome — come right in! Come right in and sit down!'

Over his shoulder, Christopher caught a hasty glimpse of a tremendous parcel of fox furs, heavy paint and hennaed hair. He fled through the workshop, and after he had seen the bookkeeper and had talked to several of the other girls, he faced the realization that it was not only with him that Ruth had been uncommunicative about her past.

★ ★ ★

'Hello . . . hello, this is Christopher Elliot. I'm trying to locate the drayman I called about a trunk that was to be picked up at a house on Echo Road . . . yes, a trunk, a semi-wardrobe. It was to be delivered to Miss Ruth Cassell . . . Yes, that was on Monday . . . All right, I'll wait.'

He let some air into the phone booth. The driver, he saw, had quit the cab and followed him in and was ostensibly drinking a Coca-Cola while eyeing him speculatively as if he wondered what the game was.

'Hello . . . are you the man I talked to? Yes, about a trunk at the white cottage on Echo Road.' He swung the booth door shut, and the next instant he was sitting bolt upright.

'You *what?*' Christopher shouted hoarsely. 'You say there was no trunk there? That's impossible! I put it on the steps myself, just before I called you . . .'

When at last Christopher stepped from the booth, he was white and shaking.

★ ★ ★

He haunted the telephone. He called hotels, rooming houses, hospitals. He developed a formula: 'I'm trying to locate a young woman, age about twenty-five. She has a cut on her chin and a bad bruise on the left side of her face; her hands and feet are cut and scratched. Her name is Ruth Cassell, but she may not be using it. She might be a victim of amnesia.'

He got nowhere.

He lost all track of time. He knew it was very late; he was now in the office and the others had left hours ago. He had avoided them as best he could. He could not avoid Margaret, but when she saw how haggard he was she let him alone.

The place was cold and he shouted to the janitor for heat. The light was on in the window on the fifth floor rear and he was suspicious of it. He added a request for information to his shout for heat, and when he learned from the janitor that an accountant named Feeley occupied that office, he called Feeley on the telephone.

The answering voice of Feeley was not the voice of Axelrod.

He felt a fool. To cover himself he lamely asked if Feeley would mind calling him at eleven. He lost track of the hours sometimes, he explained, and he didn't want to miss his train. Feeley said he'd be glad to oblige only he was quitting at ten-thirty; if it was all the same to him he'd call him then.

Relieved, Christopher agreed. It was no

matter to him when he was called. He had no train to make, nowhere to go, nothing to do but wait.

Wait, for what?

Work littered his desk. He was so tired he could not see it. Photographs, drawings, countless scraps of paper on which he had pencilled minute notes which he couldn't read. She might be at such-and-such a place, it occurred to him as he was calling somewhere else, and so as not to forget it he wrote it down.

Tomorrow, he promised himself, I am going to the police.

The police? What would they care how he had messed up his life? What solid honest cop would believe or give a damn about a cat on the telephone and a couple of dead mice?

Maybe, bud, she isn't calling you because she doesn't want to see you. You told her you were through with her, didn't you, bud? You didn't answer any of her calls before, did you, bud? So what are you all steamed up about? Whaddaya think the police department is, bud, a date bureau or somethin'?

Christopher cradled his head in his arms. Numbly he wondered what Henrietta's reaction had been when she read his confession. Angry, incredulous — no, not incredulous. She knew. Was it she who had hired the detective? Trust a woman to pick a bounder. But would she have done such a thing? If she wanted any evidence she certainly had it now. His written statement would satisfy any court in the land. *Henrietta Elliot versus Christopher Elliot; petitioner charges infidelity, insufferable indignities and intolerable cruelty and prays the court —*

The telephone rang.

He stirred in annoyance — *and prays the court grant a divorce together with custody of two minor children —*

The telephone rang again.

He roused himself, reached out a shaky hand and croaked, 'Hello — Donath and Elliot.'

'Chris?'

He came wide awake. 'In heaven's name, where are you? Where have you been? I've been almost crazy, phoning hospitals, hotels, rooming houses — you said you'd call me!'

'I know. I'm sorry.' Her voice was listless, tired. 'I had made up my mind that I wouldn't bother you again, ever.'

'Bother me?' He brought himself under control. 'It's a little late for that now. It's happened to me.' He paused, eyes narrowed, senses alert. 'The cat and mouse, I mean. Last night, at home.'

She was silent for a long moment. Then she said, 'So now you know how it feels.'

He was holding a pencil. His fingers tightened and the pencil snapped like a matchstick. He sucked in breath and asked, 'Where are you?'

'In a drugstore on Ward Avenue. I hate to bother you, Chris, but I'd like to borrow a little money. I've made up my mind to go home. I think it would be best. If you could let me have ten or fifteen dollars — I'm down to my last one.'

'Of course I'll help you. Perhaps your decision is best; maybe you should go home, at least for a while. Is the — are you being followed, do you know?'

'Possibly. I don't care. It doesn't bother me anymore.'

'It bothers me. I'd like to know. I'd like just one look at him. If I could find out who he is — ' He glanced into the areaway and up to the lighted window. 'Where did you say you were?'

'On Ward Avenue, in the seventy-two hundred block.'

'You say you have a dollar; that's enough for taxi fare. Now, listen carefully. You remember how you shook him off by going through the restaurant into C Street? I want you to take a taxi to the restaurant and come exactly the same way. When you reach C, instead of turning toward Grant go down toward the station until you reach Putnam Place. Turn right on Putnam and go straight through until you come to the first street to your right, and then it's only a block to my office. Can you remember that?'

'Down C to Putnam, turn right and then right again. Yes, Chris.'

'Good. When you reach the building come straight in and walk up the stairs — you know where the office is. The windows will be dark, but I'll be watching the street. If he's following you I'll be able to see him. Do you have it all straight, now?'

'I think so . . . yes, I've got it straight. I'll start right away. There's a cabstand out front.'

'All right. I'll have coffee and sandwiches waiting and I'll take you back in a cab, if you wish.'

'That won't be necessary. Thank you, Chris.'

He replaced the telephone and stood up. His weariness fell from him like a discarded coat. He moved past the areaway, seeing that Feeley's light held lonely vigil, and put on topcoat and hat. In the outer office he extinguished lights, crossed to the outside door and drew the spring bolt, securing it with the thumb latch. Then he ran lightly across the hall and down the stairs. When he reached the bottom he stood against the grillwork that protected the lift shaft and called down.

'Miggs!'

There was a stirring below; the scrape of a chair and the rattle of a newspaper.

'Yes, Mr. Elliot?' The voice was faintly hostile.

'I'm expecting a visitor. I'm going out for coffee but I should be back in plenty of time. Just in case I haven't returned before she arrives, the office is unlocked.'

'Yes, Mr. Elliot.'

'By the way, what time do you have? I seem to've forgotten to wind my watch.'

'I make it a quarter 'til ten, Mr. Elliot.'

5

He stood hesitant in the wide, bare hall, looking confusedly about. He did not know just where he wanted to go, and he had never been here before. A uniformed patrolman noticed his uncertainty and stepped over to him.

'Can I help you?'

'Yes, you certainly can. Where do I go if I want to find someone, and all the ordinary methods have failed?'

The patrolman backed up. 'You mean a missing person, sir?'

'Well, yes and no. I was talking to this person on the telephone last night; an appointment was made and . . . wasn't kept.' He sighed. 'Under ordinary circumstances that wouldn't be cause for alarm, but in this instance — ' He shook his head.

'You're right, sir. It doesn't pay to take chances. You go straight down this hall,' the patrolman pointed, 'then take the first hall to your right, and it's the first door on your left.'

'I — thank you, Officer. Thank you very much.'

He moved along. He was conscious of a subdued bustle within these walls, a feeling of suppressed violence that both awed and frightened him. Like many another man of his class, he took law enforcement for granted, basing his judgment of the police department either on fiction or movies or the patrolman he met on the street.

But now that he was in the heart of it, he was suddenly terrified.

He stood before a desk, addressing a fleshy and extremely important-looking person. He had a story to tell, but the fleshy person wouldn't let him tell it in his own way. There was a form to be filled out. Name, age, height, weight, race, sex, nationality, home address, business address, occupation, when last seen, what wearing when last seen —

'I don't know! I told you I hadn't seen her in a week!'

Complexion, colour of eyes and hair,

identifying marks, moles, pigmentations, deformities —

'When I last saw her the whole left side of her face was bruised. She had a cut on her chin. Her hands and feet were cut and scratched.'

The fleshy man stopped writing. 'Just a minute,' he said and vanished into a door. After what seemed an interminable wait, he reappeared.

He waved a fat hand. 'In here.'

It wasn't a request; it was a command.

★　★　★

The small office was filled with a littered desk, a battered filing cabinet, a few straight chairs, and a rickety coat rack. Its narrow limits were defined by partitions built of matched boards, stained dark, to chair height and of dingy pebbled glass above. Beyond the partition to the left a typewriter clacked busily; on the right a low-hanging light fixture made a rising widespread sun against the rough thick glass.

The air here was charged with tension;

he had felt it growing as he followed in the wheezing, waddling wake of the fleshy man. He had come down a long corridor, up steps and to the left to a plain glass-panelled door with no identifying sign on it. The instant that the door had closed behind him and he had been left alone, to sit and wait, he had regretted coming to this place.

He was lighting a cigarette when the door at his left opened to admit a man who, because of his height and breadth, appeared at first to be alone. But when he moved aside he revealed a slim little woman who quietly crossed the room and unobtrusively occupied one of the straight chairs.

At sight of the stenographer's pad and pencil in the woman's hands, Christopher bristled.

'Is that necessary?' he demanded.

The large man seated himself at the desk. He had a moustache, and his answering smile served to reveal startlingly white teeth. 'Sometimes it's advisable, Mr. Elliot. A man is usually more careful of what he says when he knows it's being taken down.' His voice was deep and faintly musical. 'This is Miss McGhee,' his dark head, frosted at the temples, inclined to the woman, 'and I'm Joe Dickerson.'

Dickerson. Christopher eyed him thoughtfully. Vaguely he remembered having heard of this man. He said, 'I'm a little bit overwhelmed at all this. I seem to have got in here easily enough. Now I wonder how I'm going to get out.'

Dickerson laughed. 'You needn't be alarmed. I asked you to come in here because I gather that you are looking for help. I thought we might clear the usual red tape and save you some time. You may speak in confidence. Tell the story any way you like. I believe you are trying to find someone, a woman.'

'I am. I'd been trying to locate her for several days, and last night, at a little after half-past nine, she telephoned me at my office. She said she would get a cab and come straight down, but she never showed up. It was after midnight when I gave up waiting for her.'

146

'I see. And you tried to contact her this morning and couldn't find her, so you came to us. Is that it?'

'That,' Christopher sighed, 'is it.'

Dickerson touched his lower teeth to his moustache. 'You say she telephoned you. Any idea where she telephoned from?'

'She said she was calling from a drugstore in the seventy-two hundred block on Ward Avenue; she said there was a cabstand in front, and she would leave there at once. I went to the drugstore this morning, and I talked with some of the cab drivers at the stand, but none of them seemed to remember her.'

'And she would have been rather easy to spot, of course, because of the bruises on her face.'

Christopher flushed. 'You seem to know something about her.'

Dickerson blandly waved a large hand. 'I have your partially filled-out missing person's report, Mr. Elliot. You say you waited for her until after midnight. Did you leave your office at any time? Could she have possibly arrived there during

147

your absence, and not finding you in, gone away again?'

Christopher frowned in thought. 'I left directly after she called, but I was gone only a few minutes. I told Miggs, the janitor, that I expected her and to look out for her. I was gone only long enough to cross the street to an all-night restaurant and get some coffee and sandwiches. When I returned, Miggs said she hadn't arrived yet and I wasn't alarmed because I knew she had a longish way to come. But as time wore on I became worried. At a quarter past ten, I think it was, a man named Feeley, an accountant on the fifth floor of the building, called me because I had asked him to give me a ring when he was leaving — sometimes I lose track of time when I'm working — and somewhere around eleven Miggs called up the lift shaft to ask if I'd need him for anything because he was going to bed.' Christopher exhaled.

Dickerson leaned back frowning. 'It doesn't seem very logical that you could have missed her. Do you suppose she might have changed her mind suddenly? Women sometimes do, you know.'

'Not in this case. She was coming to borrow some money. Thinking that something might have happened, such as a taxi accident, to delay her, I put the money in an envelope, woke up poor Miggs and instructed him to give it to her in case she should arrive later. But this morning Miggs told me he waited until after two, when he fell asleep. That was when I really became alarmed; thinking she might have been in an accident I called the hospitals, without any success. Then I went out to Ward Avenue as I told you.'

Dickerson chewed thoughtfully at his moustache. He sat quietly a moment, apparently absorbed in thought, and such was her ability to efface herself that Christopher abruptly remembered the presence of the woman. She sat, patient and immobile, head bent and pencil ready; she acted neither interested nor bored in the proceedings.

Dickerson said, 'It's rather unusual, isn't it, for the loaner to seek the would-be borrower? I'd like to know more of the circumstances, Mr. Elliot. If you really want to find this woman, and I assume that you do, I'll have to know more about her. You had been trying to find her for several days, but couldn't. Why not? Obviously she wasn't trying to avoid you, or she wouldn't have telephoned. Why did she call you at your office at that hour? Why not at your home? Why did she want to borrow money, and why go to you for it? Just what is your connection with her?'

'She — ' Christopher paused. His glance swept to the patient, bent figure of Miss McGhee, and when it returned to Dickerson it held pleading.

Dickerson's grey eyes were unwaveringly direct. 'Mr. Elliot,' he said quietly, 'Miss McGhee is my most trusted and valued assistant. You must realize that a great many people have sat in that chair and have brought problems to me as you are now bringing yours. The notes that Miss McGhee takes down help us to help you. Questions sometimes arise; I do not have too good a memory. If I can refer to the notes, it saves a great deal of my time and of yours. I want to assure you that you can trust Miss McGhee fully as much as you can trust me; if you do not feel that you trust me, we are both wasting our time.'

Christopher eyed him thoughtfully. Joe Dickerson; Lieutenant Dickerson, that was it. He had heard of this man. His name cropped up every so often in newspaper accounts. He recalled now having seen his picture in a national magazine. All the memories he could summon of him were reassuring, and the cumulative impression was that this man could be trusted.

Within Christopher, a gate let down suddenly.

He had not realized how tired and alone and in need of help he was. Suddenly it came pouring out: the whole incredible business of the cat and mouse, that unexpected and unwanted dividend of his hapless affair with Ruth Cassell.

When he had covered the events of the previous day, up to the time of Ruth's telephone call, he was spent and shaking.

Dickerson found him a cup of coffee somewhere, and gave him a cigarette. Miss McGhee left them, and when she had gone Dickerson said, slowly, 'That cat and mouse business, Mr. Elliot. I don't like it.'

The coffee warmed Christopher and brought him back a little. 'I didn't like it either, Lieutenant. Perhaps you can imagine how I felt.'

'I can. It smacks of insanity. We've been up against maniacs before. They're not always hard to catch, but the time factor is against us. Sometimes they can do a lot of damage before we put them away — ' He frowned. 'The drayman said that when he reached the cottage the trunk wasn't there?'

'Absolutely. He might be lying. He might have forgotten to go. It's possible that the trunk is still there, on the flagstone steps, unless someone has stolen it by now.'

'I'm not so sure, Mr. Elliot. The drayman might be telling the truth. It may be that between the time when you left the cottage and he arrived at it someone had removed the trunk. We can check on him. The law requires him to maintain a trip record, and if he failed to go on that run we'll soon know about it.'

Dickerson got up from his chair. His florid face held concern. 'Could you identify this girl if you saw her?'

'Certainly. I knew her very well. I — I told you about us.'

Dickerson depressed the lever of the interphone on his desk. 'McGhee, if anyone wants me I'll be back shortly. Tell Connelly to stand by. I'll have some work for him.' He quit the desk and turned to Christopher. 'Would you come with me? I think you won't have much longer to wait.'

⋆　⋆　⋆

The room was large and cold and it held a faint, irritating smell. Along one wall of it there were numbered compartments and as Christopher progressed, with each advancing step the cold penetrated further within him.

Other men had joined Dickerson. One

was small and cheerful, smelling weakly of cigars and strongly of liquor. Another was young, long-faced, seriously intent, hugging to Dickerson and the small man as if fearful of missing a single word.

'Try one-seventeen,' the small cheerful man said. 'I think that's the one.'

They deviated to the left. From behind pillars still another man appeared. He bore an armload and he announced to no one in particular, 'These are the clothes.'

Dickerson selected an item from the pile. He turned, holding up a fur-trimmed, fawn-coloured coat. He held it by the shoulders, shaking it out until it was full length. On one side of it, the side with the buttons, a heavy dark stain surrounded a small burned hole in the fabric.

'Recognize this, Mr. Elliot?' Dickerson asked.

Christopher looked at it numbly, and some power greater than himself caused him to shudder. He nodded slowly.

'One-seventeen?' The serious youth turned from the compartment to the blatantly cheerful small man. 'Here. I'll help you roll it out — easy, easy — there.'

The man with the clothing whistled. 'Say, not bad. Not bad at all.'

Dickerson pushed them aside, almost angrily it seemed. He straightened and turned respectfully. 'Would you mind looking at her for a second, Mr. Elliot?'

Christopher's fascinated eyes reluctantly quit the coat with its tell-tale stain, wavered and, avoiding the slab, glanced at the marble floor. He could not force himself to look at her face. He began to tremble. Suddenly he felt weak and ill and somehow unaccountably old. Slowly he nodded his head and turned away.

Brief silence held behind him. Then a shoe scraped on the marble floor. There was the heavy sound of rollers and the *chock* of the door as it fell to.

The fellow with the clothing came by, carelessly folding the coat on top of the pile, and as he reached the pillars he began whistling 'Gotta Be This or That'.

Dickerson stepped away. 'All right,' he said. 'Name: Ruth Cassell. We'll have the rest of it later. Identification established

by Christopher Elliot — ' the briefest
appreciable pause, ' — close friend.'

★ ★ ★

They were in Dickerson's office again. It
was quieter now; the clacking of the
typewriter was stilled and the bustle of
the building had receded to a subdued
hum. They were alone together and it was
some minutes before Christopher could
find his voice.

'Was there a mouse?' The unexpected
harshness of his voice startled him.

'A mouse?' Dickerson glanced up from
a typescript on his desk. A faintly puzzled
expression cleared from his eyes. 'No, Mr.
Elliot. No mice. No cats. Nothing fancy.
Just a slug through the heart.' He put the
typescript down, and while he weighed
Christopher with his eyes he touched his
moustache with his lower teeth.

'Mr. Elliot, there are certain points in
your statement which need clarification. I
realize that you have just suffered a grave
shock, but I'm sure you'll agree with me
that, under circumstances as they now

stand, we must have all the information we can possibly get. Do you feel up to answering a few questions?'

'Frankly, I don't know. I'm not sure if I could give you intelligent answers right now.'

'Please try. It's important. How long had you known Ruth Cassell altogether?'

'About eight or nine months. No more than that.'

'Do you know where she came from, who her parents or any of her relatives are, who any of her associates might be?'

Christopher shook his head. 'No.'

'Can you think of anyone who might know?'

'Possibly Marge Donath. They were in college together. Marge is in Reno at the present time, at a dude ranch, I think.'

'We'll contact her — now, about this Axelrod. He called you only the one time?'

'That's all.

'Do you have any idea who he might be, or who might have hired him?'

'No.'

'You were to call him tonight?'

'Yes.'

'We'll check that too. The mouse, the one your daughter had. You took it for analysis?'

'Yes, to Doctor Swinburne, a pathologist in the Professional Arts Building. I haven't had a chance to see him again for the report.'

'I'll have it picked up.' Dickerson frowned and worried his moustache. 'Now, Mr. Elliot, I don't want you to take offence at what I'm about to ask you; I'm only trying to get some sense out of this damned cat and mouse business. While you were having your affair with Ruth Cassell, do you know what your wife was doing?'

Christopher reddened. 'I don't believe I understand you.'

'I think you do. While you were neglecting her she might have turned to someone else for companionship. Who among your friends would be eligible? Donath? Brokaw? Ashton?'

'Really, Lieutenant. If you knew Henrietta at all you'd realize how impossible the idea is. But as for the ones you've mentioned: Bill Donath is a dipsomaniac, and Henrietta has never been cordial to him. She detests Arthur Brokaw. And as for Lyman Ashton: she thinks him amusing, but he is trying his best to impress Cissie Folwell with his desirability. No, Lieutenant. You're wrong.'

Dickerson stood up abruptly. 'I'm sorry for you, Mr. Elliot. I believe you were really fond of the girl, but you must realize that on the strength of your admissions we have to hold you for questioning.'

Christopher faced him with dismay. 'You — you've tricked me!'

'I wouldn't say so. There are no damaging admissions in your statement. Eventually we would have identified her, and we would have learned about you. But from now on I advise you to be very careful what you say.'

★ ★ ★

The light annoyed him, although it did not shine directly into his eyes unless he attempted to see beyond it, to try to

159

fathom who was questioning him at the moment. The positions of the light and the chair he sat in were arranged so that he could not see who it was or how many of them there were, unless he caught the full glare of the light.

The chair bothered him considerably more. Two inches or so had been purposely sawed from a back leg; when first he had sat down he had feared he would go over backwards to the floor. It was difficult to balance on the three good legs. Sometimes he forgot and leaned back and the result was torture.

His ideas of police procedure had been formed from few authentic sources. When he learned he was to be questioned he had been certain he would be subjected to the light, and he had thought that they might beat him with a length of rubber hose or blow cigarette smoke in his face or place a glass of water tantalizingly out of reach.

He quickly discovered how false some of his preconceptions were.

He had not anticipated being minutely gone over with a vacuum cleaner. The nozzle sucked his clothing away from his skin, tugged at pockets, trouser cuffs, socks and hair, and the buzzing motor made his flesh itch as if with hives. He had been certain he would be fingerprinted, but he had not even vaguely imagined they would scrape beneath his fingernails, swab his nostrils, dig into his ears, and measure and photograph the stubborn, unhealing cut on his hand.

Or that they would measure and photograph him, force him to walk under brilliant lights on a narrow stage against a backdrop of horizontal lines, one in a file of nondescripts passing in review before an unseen audience.

Nor was that all. He was told that under the law he could not be forced to give a sample of his blood; it was his right to refuse and his refusal would in no way jeopardize him. But they wanted it. Would he mind?

Tiredly he nodded, scratched his name to a consent paper and they opened a vein.

Anger, he found, got him nowhere.

That was their game. They would pass and interpass behind the light, baiting, badgering and trying to trick him. They tried to make him admit to depravities and practices of which he had never heard. He thought at first this business of hurling totally unrelated accusations at him was sheer sadistic stupidity; later he was less sure. He began to detect the threads of a pattern and could almost feel the net they were trying to draw around him.

There were different voices, different men, different and confusing questions being hurled at him from shifting positions behind the light. But one voice, one shadowy substance held to a theme which never varied. Always quiet, insinuating, at times faintly amused, it was this one who was weaving the fabric. Why did you kill her? You had nothing to gain. You knew you couldn't get away with it. *Why did you kill her?*

He came to know and hate that voice.

The voice was not Dickerson's. He could not even be sure if Dickerson was in the room. If Dickerson was there he did not speak. It was a terrible strain, listening and being prepared for a voice which never came.

In the beginning he was sometimes angry, but he became progressively cooler. He answered questions with the degree of civility that the question merited. At first he answered painfully and at length; when, with the passage of time, he found them repeating again and again, he shortened his answers until they became little more than 'yes' or 'no' or 'I don't know.'

How long he could have continued he did not know. He did not know that he was near exhaustion when some maniacal clown amongst them started meowing like a cat.

From then on they got nothing from him at all.

You don't grill a man like Christopher Elliot for too long, and you don't hold him for too long, either. In the morning they permitted him to call Ed Kaufman and in an hour he was free.

*   *   *

To be out of the closure of walls and breathe the outer air like other men; to ride in a cab and be protected from photographers and then be whisked upward in a two-step into the comfortable sanctuary of an apartment where the only lights were friendly things to see and read by, and the only voices were civilized, respectful and reassuring.

Kaufman was a wonder.

When Christopher stepped from the luxury of a steaming shower and a shave into an inviting bedroom he found spread out for him a complete change of clothing. Clean socks, underwear and a shirt, all in the proper size; a suit of blue-striped worsted that might have been tailored for him; a choice of neckwear, handkerchiefs, and even a new hat which combined both the proper head size and the style he preferred.

He felt no elation. He had come too far to receive satisfaction from material things. But he was especially glad for the hat. It reassured him. He had feared Kaufman might want to keep him cooped up. He wanted to be free. He wanted latitude.

Death had ended Ruth Cassell's problems. Never again would she tremble at the presence of an unknown behind her, listen fascinated to the wail of a cat or flee in terror from a mouse on her pillow. The hand which had struck her down had in truth performed an act of mercy. But for Christopher Elliot the Living, tied to this dead woman by these incomprehensible bonds of cat and mouse, her death was but a milestone on a shrouded road.

Kaufman was waiting for him in the library. The lawyer's shrewd eyes appraised him swiftly, yet with disconcerting thoroughness. Kaufman, in his long career, had been called many things both complimentary and otherwise, but there were none who would deny either his shrewdness or his thoroughness.

'You'll do,' Kaufman said. 'Feeling better?'

'Much, thanks to you,' Christopher nodded. He regarded his counsellor thoughtfully and again wondered, as had so many before him, how this man who looked so much like a farmer could be so successful in the devious furrows of the law. He supposed Kaufman would want to hear his side of the story. He asked, 'When do we start?'

'All in due time.' Kaufman fiddled with an enormous elk's tooth on his heavy gold watch-chain. 'Lunch will be ready in about twenty minutes. There are some questions I'll want to ask. First and most important is: did you kill her?'

'No!'

'Take it easy. That'll help some. You understand the spot you're in. When the police have a prime, made-to-order suspect like you, especially since you're a prominent man, they've got something the newspapers will lap up. Everybody from the beat cop who found her all the way up to the commissioner has a chance to get his mug in the news pictures. We're lucky in one respect. Joe Dickerson is conscientious and he's honest. If you didn't knock the girl off, and Dickerson can find anything to convince him that you didn't, he won't try to frame you.

How much did you spill to him?'

'All of it.'

Kaufman scowled. 'I wish you'd called me yesterday. We could have saved ourselves a hell of a lot of trouble.'

'I didn't know about it yesterday. I went there to report her as missing. I didn't know she was dead, although I guess I should have suspected it. But I didn't know until Dickerson took me to the morgue. That was after I had told him the whole story.'

Kaufman rubbed his nose reflectively. 'We don't have to worry too much about the third-degree, not if you're innocent. Did you let them test your blood?'

'I wish you'd stop saying 'if'! Of course I let them test my blood!'

'Take it easy. We've got a long way to go. It won't make much difference. The state doesn't allow blood in evidence anyway. It's just one of Joe Dickerson's ideas.' Kaufman chuckled. 'I'll bet you gave 'em a bad time at the inquisition.'

'They gave me a bad time.'

'It's all an act. Effective with morons and neurasthenics, but the stuff that comes out of it never gets anywhere in court. In the hands of the proper defence, even signed confessions are a dime a dozen. And eyewitnesses can be crossed up, confused and made to appear ridiculous. But physical evidence, the silent witness, is something else entirely. Dickerson knows it, and that's where he'll make his drive.'

'The silent witness?'

'Buttons, dust, hair, thread, fibres: anything that can place the killer at the scene of the crime.'

'Then I've got nothing to worry about.'

Kaufman dangled the elk's tooth moodily. 'You have nothing really serious to worry about,' he corrected emphatically. 'Innocent or guilty, you're in for a bad time, Elliot. While we're waiting for lunch I'll give you an outline of what we've got to do. First, I'll want you to repeat to me the same story you gave Dickerson, as nearly the same as you can possibly make it. If anything has occurred to you or has happened since, you can save it until later. But the statement you gave to Dickerson must be exactly so.

'Now, here's what will happen. With identification established the investigation is already well underway. Your questioning was only one phase of it; while his staff was working on you, Joe Dickerson was organizing other lines. The coroner's physician has performed the post mortem and the vital organs have been sent to the pathologist; the bullet has been extracted and turned over to ballistics. Findings will be reported to the coroner's jury which will probably meet this afternoon. If Dickerson's found any sort of witnesses, their testimony will be taken and beyond any reasonable doubt the jury will render a verdict of homicide at the hands of a person or persons unknown.

'From there it goes to the grand jury. Dickerson will be called in to present his evidence. If his evidence points strongly enough to us or to anyone else, a true bill of indictment will be returned by name, and if we should happen to be on it we'll just have to stew in the can until time for our appearance at the superior court. That gives us time to organize and conduct an investigation of our own. I have a couple of men who have been out on it already, but we have to be careful. They can give us a bad time for obstructing justice — '

Kaufman paused and his eyes became sharply direct. 'It will cost money, Elliot. For that reason I've made arrangements for a supplementary office for you where you can work without being disturbed. There are only three things I want from you: I want your complete honesty and co-operation, I want you to tend to business and leave the job of investigation to the police and to me, and before we go any further I want a retainer of five thousand dollars. If you don't have that much cash on hand, I'll take what you can spare and a note for the balance.'

★ ★ ★

After Christopher had completed, to the best of his memory, a reiteration of the statement he had made to Dickerson, he found Kaufman was considerably less sympathetic than Dickerson had been.

'How do you know the girl heard this

cat sound over the telephone?'

'She told me she did.'

'Then why didn't you tell Dickerson she told you instead of making the positive statement that she had heard it? And the mouse — why did you drop it in the toilet? Why didn't you keep it? Do you realize how preposterous the whole thing must have sounded to a man like Dickerson?'

'He didn't act as if it sounded preposterous. I don't care how it sounded. It's the truth.'

'Don't you realize how they've got you tied? You cut your hand when you were opening the rear door of the cottage; you dumped the glass in the waste basket. Your blood was on that glass, yet you permitted them to take a sample from you.'

'It was probably foolish of me, but — '

'Foolish? The girl's feet were cut! She bled while she was in your car! They'll have that by now. Do you know what it adds up to?'

'No.'

'Regardless of your story, they'll think

you gave her a beating. Not that it means a hell of a lot what they think, but it all builds up. You were doing everything you could to get rid of her. She was threatening your home life and happiness. You beat the bejesus out of her and she still wouldn't go. So you removed her.'

Christopher arose unsteadily. 'If you're going to keep this up, Kaufman, we'll stop now. I hired you to defend me, not to tear me to pieces.'

Kaufman's manner changed instantly. 'Sit down, son. Let me tell you something. You told me you didn't kill the girl. I believe you. If that was all it amounted to you could walk out of here a free man, free to patch up your life as best you could. But I want you to realize that you are on trial, not only under the processes of the law, but also in the eyes of your family and friends. You've got to accept the fact. You can't go to them with a chip on your shoulder. Because of your involvement in the death of this girl your wife is in a hell of a spot. Maybe, in spite of the act that caused her to leave you, she'd like to reconsider now. But there will be pressure. Her family will want to shield her from further embarrassment. *Your* friends will suddenly become *her* friends. Don't you see it?'

'I see only that you think I killed Ruth Cassell.'

Kaufman spread his hands. 'You're the most obstinate damned fool I ever saw.' Suddenly he leaned forward and his face became a savage mask. 'You didn't kill the girl. All right, you didn't. Then someone else did. That someone's motives could very well have been influenced by your conduct and intimacy with the girl. It is not beyond the realm of possibility that this someone saw her bruises, deduced therefrom that you had beaten her, and now that she has been removed, the someone might as easily want to remove you. Don't you see that because of the circumstances, possibly the only way we can establish your innocence will be by establishing the guilt of this other person, the real killer? And I'm damned if I want a situation where I've got to take your carcass into court to prove that you are not the murderer!'

Christopher sat down. 'The newspapers,' he said thickly. 'Let me see them.'

Kaufman's mien changed again. He chuckled. 'You can read the newspapers after a while, and when you are reading them try to remember that you've probably read worse. The difference is that you're on the other side of the fence this time. Now, tell me . . . '

6

Lieutenant Joseph Dickerson stepped to the exact centre of the worn green carpet, stiffened to attention and said, 'You sent for me, sir?'

The commissioner glanced up from a report he was reading. Scowling, he waved a hand as large and hairy as a coconut.

'Sit down, Dickerson.'

The lieutenant drew up a chair and sat defensively on the forward third of it. 'Is anything wrong, sir?'

'Wrong?' The commissioner eyed him. 'I don't always call you up here because something's gone wrong. Sometimes I want to stop things before they have a chance to go wrong.'

'You mean the Cassell case, sir?'

'That's what I mean. Don't you and your trained seals know this man Elliot isn't common people? You can't push him around like you would some two-bit punk from Docktown. Now I see he's hired Ed Kaufman. When Kaufman gets through with us we'll be bleeding from the ears.'

'I've done nothing to Elliot.'

'Nothing?' the commissioner bellowed. 'You call putting him through the wringer nothing?' He glared indignantly. Then he relaxed suddenly, his voice dropped to normal and he asked anxiously, 'How'd he show up? Got anything on him?'

'We have plenty on him. Too much.'

'Too much?'

'Yes, sir. I don't like it. This cat and mouse business, I mean. It sounds like the work of a maniac, and Elliot's a long way from being that.'

'D'you suppose he could be rigging us? D'you think there really are a cat and a mouse mixed up in it?'

'There's a mouse, all right. And his wife verifies the midnight phone call, although whether he heard a cat crying is another question. But the little girl had something in her hands; Elliot took it from her and that was what brought his home troubles to a head. Mrs. Elliot said the little girl told her it was a mouse, and since she'd been sleeping in Elliot's bed at the time, Mrs. Elliot supposes the mouse must have been under his pillow. It doesn't seem possible anyone could've entered the room with both of them sleeping there, so the mouse might have been under the pillow all day. In fact,' Dickerson frowned, 'Elliot might have put it there himself, but he certainly acts sane to me. It's a puzzle all right, that part of it.'

'What happened to the mouse?'

'Elliot took it to a commercial pathologist. We have his report. The mouse died of carbon monoxide poisoning.'

'Hah!' The commissioner scratched his chin. 'I've been in the business a long time, Dickerson, but this mouse angle is a new one to me. What about the rest of Elliot's story?'

'We went over the cottage on Echo Road, Chelmere. We found blood, a lot of it. We can't use blood types in court, but it does help us with our investigation. Elliot's a type O and the girl was an AB. We found spatters of O in the kitchen near the door and on broken glass in the wastebasket. There was AB on the kitchen porch, kitchen floor, in the living room, bedroom and bathroom and, more to the point, on the seat and floor of Elliot's car. These findings substantiate his story about what went on at the cottage and on the road Sunday night.

'But we haven't yet located the trunk he said he packed for her on Monday. There was such a trunk; we checked with the janitor of the apartment house. Also we checked the truckman's trip tickets and he did go to the cottage within an hour of Elliot's call, but the trunk had disappeared in the meantime. We'll turn it up eventually; it's only a matter of time.

'And as if that wasn't enough, Elliot told us a man named Axelrod had tried to shake him down by telephone. He was supposed to call a number last night and give a message to the effect that he was ready to pay off. We had the phone company put a monitor on the line and we had a man there. At eleven o'clock last night someone telephoned and asked if there were any messages for Mr. Axelrod. We traced the call to a telephone booth in a Ward Avenue drugstore. We used the block system and a radio car was there within three minutes, but the booth was empty and no one in the drugstore could give us any sort of description. We know it couldn't have been Elliot because at that time Elliot was in the tank.'

The commissioner pawed at his generous chin. 'Hah. How about the place where she was found?'

'A filthy alley about two blocks from the place where Elliot was supposedly waiting for her. We've checked his alibi and it holds up; the counterman in the Busy Bee remembers him, the janitor won't be apt to forget him, and an accountant named Feeley swears he called Elliot fifteen minutes before he was supposed to. Oh, his time is pretty well accounted for. Still — ' Dickerson frowned.

'What was in the envelope Elliot left for the janitor, the one he was supposed to give the girl?'

'Fifteen dollars in cash and a note saying *Before you go, call me at the City Club or my office. I've got to talk to you.*'

'Hmph. If it was so important, why didn't he wait?'

'He'd had no sleep for forty-eight hours. A man can take just so much and then he'll fold unless he uses stimulants. Elliot will hardly touch a drink since his friend Donath hit the skids. Donath's divorce, incidentally, was the cause of Elliot's breaking it off with Ruth Cassell.'

'Hm-umph.' Pursuit of involved relationships was admittedly not one of the commissioner's strongpoints. He liked something he could put his finger on. 'Did you get anything worthwhile out of the autopsy?'

Dickerson frowned thoughtfully. 'The external examination showed no new bruises, and the scratch test gave us nothing. There was a minute quantity of a foreign substance on her lips; we don't yet know what it was, but the lab is working on it. But the closest scrutiny of corpse and clothing failed to reveal any extraneous hairs, fibres, threads, dust or other matter foreign to the woman or to the place where she was found.

'She was shot from in front from such

close range the gas explosion tore away the apex of the heart. There was fragmentation of the bullet; total weight of lead particles twenty-seven grains. Taken with the lubrication, smokeless load and non-corrosive primer we reconstruct the bullet to be a high velocity hollow point twenty-two short, a very deadly slug at close range. The small amount of noise made by the cartridge accounts for the fact that we've been unable to locate anyone who heard the shot.

'The rest of it doesn't amount to much. Alcohol, alkaloids and toxics negative. Condition of the stomach would indicate she had eaten very little and this with the presence of only twenty-five cents in her handbag — she'd made the appointment with Elliot for the purpose of borrowing money — suggests that she was in desperate financial circumstances.

'The coroner's physician estimates the time of death as somewhere between ten and ten-thirty p.m. He also estimates that she died within a few minutes of the attack. I have one witness who saw her walk through Lumson's Chop House at approximately ten o'clock; there were others who noticed her but none of them seemed to have any clear idea of what time it was.

'And that,' Dickerson frowned, 'brings us to Mr. Elliot. I have timed the distance from his office to where Ruth Cassell's body was found. I walked it myself, without hurrying, in less than three minutes. Since he had directed her, knew when she was leaving and the exact route she would follow he could probably guess fairly accurately when she would arrive. All he had to do was walk towards her, and in not over ten minutes he could have returned to the Busy Bee, bought his coffee and sandwiches and gone back to his office, ostensibly to wait.

'It sounds easy, but there are plenty of holes in it.

'When Elliot left Chelmere Tuesday morning the only suit he had with him was the one he had on; he was wearing it when he showed up here. It must, therefore, have been the same suit he was wearing the night Ruth Cassell was killed.

We gave his clothing every test there is and he came off absolutely clean.

'But even so he might possibly have escaped receiving powder marks or blood spatters since the pistol was held against her body and the folds of her coat acted as a muffler.

'An inch-by-inch search of the area has failed to produce the pistol. We've searched Elliot's offices and building, his room at the City Club, sewers, manholes, trash and garbage cans. We did find one pistol in Elliot's desk, but it was the wrong calibre; his secretary said it had belonged to the senior member of the firm and had been used for guarding payrolls when they were in the construction business. Since we can't find the pistol we've got to assume that either the killer is smarter at hiding than we are at finding, or else he's lugging the pistol around with him, which would eliminate Mr. Elliot.

'That brings us to Elliot's timing. He left the building at quarter to ten to go to the Busy Bee for coffee and sandwiches; the counterman at the restaurant isn't sure of the time, but he thinks Elliot left with his order sometime around ten; the janitor says Elliot brought him coffee and a sandwich and talked with him for a few minutes; we knew Feeley called him at quarter-past ten, which was fifteen minutes ahead of schedule, and we know it was midnight before he left the building again.'

The commissioner balled a hairy fist and scratched the back of it with a horny forefinger. 'All right. So much for Elliot. What else have you got?'

'Frankly, very little. That's what worries me. We haven't been able to get a thing on this Ruth Cassell, where she came from or anything about her. We do have the name of the college she attended, and the registrar is going to let us know some time today where she registered from.

'I haven't been able to locate the cab driver who brought her to Lumson's Chop House, but I have found the drugstore from which she made the telephone call. It's in the seventy-two hundred block on Ward Avenue. It happens to be the same drugstore from which our friend Axelrod called the service bureau last night.'

★ ★ ★

Connelly was waiting when Dickerson returned to his office. Connelly's ordinarily worried face was garnished with a broad smile, and the smile made him appear even more like a horse than usual.

'I turned up somethin', Chief. That coat. She bought it, along with the dress, in a shop on Grant Avenue. Monday afternoon.'

'Monday,' Dickerson repeated softly. 'You're certain it was she who bought the coat?'

'Poz, Chief. She's a regular customer there. She charged the stuff and signed for it.'

'A change of outfit. She was afraid to go back to her apartment. Was she with anyone?'

'Nope. She was alone. The clerk took especial notice of her because of that bruise on her face. The clerk watched her while she went out. She waited on the

185

corner until a Ward Avenue bus came along and she got on it.'

'Ward Avenue. It ties in with the drugstore. How many men do we have working that area?'

'Four. We can't miss. That gal was marked. We ought to have the place she was hidin' out almost any minute now.'

Dickerson gave him a significant look. 'She was marked, all right. There are some things about this that don't add up. According to Elliot, she had 'enough' money when he gave her an additional thirty dollars. If we can consider 'enough' to be as little as a ten-spot, she left Chelmere Sunday night with at least forty dollars. She spent no cash in the Grand Avenue shop, and on Wednesday night we find her down to her last quarter. We can be sure that if she was staying anywhere near the seventy-two hundred block on Ward Avenue her expenses wouldn't be over four dollars a day top. She wasn't drinking, and she was eating hardly enough to keep a canary alive.

'But let's be extravagant. Let's figure three days at six dollars a day. That amounts to eighteen. Add incidentals, bus and taxi fare of two dollars more. That accounts for only twenty dollars. What became of the rest of it?'

Connelly twisted an ear. 'Think she might've had it in her bag when she was on her way to touch Elliot? It might be she was held up. Maybe it's a heist guy we're lookin' for.'

'It might be,' Dickerson admitted. 'But she might also have turned it over to some small time chiseller, some tight-pants guy who was making her life miserable.'

In a half-hour Dickerson had his answer.

They found her room — a drably furnished cubicle in a dingy boarding-house. She had paid the landlady five dollars; what few meals she had eaten she had prepared herself. They found a half-used loaf of bread, some cold cuts and cheese and two empty milk bottles in a window box.

Personal items were pitifully few.

There was, however, a small portable phonograph. The landlady said Ruth had bought it on Monday. Dickerson lifted the lid. The only record he could find was the *Warsaw Concerto* and it was on the turntable. But he was satisfied, for now he knew almost to the penny where her money had gone.

★ ★ ★

Before leaving Kaufman's apartment, Christopher called his home. The voice that answered was masculine and utterly strange. He was baffled until insight warned him that this was either the press or the police. He guessed that Henrietta had probably gone to her mother's and so he called the Geer house, and presently was listening to Wick.

'I'm afraid Henrietta would prefer not to talk with you.' Wick's voice was drily civil. 'It shouldn't be necessary to state reasons.'

'Did she say that, or are you assuming it?'

'My dear fellow, I might resent your implication if I didn't feel a certain amount of sympathy for you. You must realize that Henrietta has seen the newspapers. Things have been most difficult for her.'

'I suppose you think they've been easy for me. Has Henrietta read the letter I left for her?'

'She didn't discuss it with me.' Wick's answer was cool. 'Lyman Ashton was here on your behalf. Since I did not intrude on the conversation and since Henrietta did not choose to reveal its context I can tell you nothing about it. I can report that since Slade induced her to take a sedative she has had more rest. Also Wickie appears to be well, but Teena, I'm sorry to say, is in a highly nervous condition.'

Teena. That was it. They would never forgive him. His eyes hardened. 'Wick, if you've read the newspapers you know the spot I'm in. I need help. There is certain information I must have. You're close to Bill Donath. I know it's a point of honour, but I must have the name of the girl, the one with whom he was involved. Can you give it to me?'

'I'm sorry.'

'Will you find out for me? I can't tell

you how important it is. There must be someone who knows, and I'm not ready to come to Chelmere yet.'

'Really, Christopher, don't you think you've carried this Donath farce about far enough?'

Christopher inhaled shakily. *Farce!* So that was what Wick thought. 'I see. You don't wish to become involved. I should have realized. Do you know if Henrietta will talk to me later today? Tonight? Tomorrow? Sometime?'

'I'll ask her, but I think you're wasting your time.'

Throughout the conversation Kaufman had been watching him. Kaufman's brow was furrowed, his head slightly bent and the elk's tooth was constantly bobbing in his fingers.

'You'd better get some rest,' Kaufman advised. 'Give your family a couple of days to cool off. Your wife will get her head. She'll come around when she's convinced herself that you need her. Women like to be big.'

He was not stopped in the lobby. The pavement was clear, and when he saw a cab standing at the curb he began to breathe more freely.

'Hotel Paulson,' he directed and settled back in the seat. He would catch up on rest some time, but first things came first. The office Kaufman had arranged for him was one of the Paulson's unused sample rooms. Margaret had arranged for Griggs and Flanders to be there. It would be a bit inconvenient, but they would manage. When he had talked to Margaret on the telephone she had chosen to act as if nothing had happened and he hoped she would keep it that way.

The cab swung into traffic, reached the intersection, did a right turn and pulled up to the curb.

'Here!' Christopher leaned forward. 'What are you doing? I said — '

The door at his right opened and he saw a man entering to occupy the seat with him. He did not recognize him at once because his head was bent and his grey snap-brimmed hat shielded his face. When he straightened, Christopher saw him to be Joe Dickerson.

'All right, Driver,' Dickerson called. The cab pulled away.

Christopher faced around. He was shaking with fury. 'Lieutenant, perhaps you can tell me the meaning of this. I've had quite enough of you. I have been released on bail. Any further dealings you have with me will be through Mr. Kaufman. Now, either you get out of this car or I will!'

Dickerson nodded seriously. 'I don't blame you in the least, Mr. Elliot. I'll admit that my method of approach was crude, and I apologize for it. But believe me, my motives are of the best.'

'I'm not interested in your motives. Driver!'

'It's no good, sir. He's a friend of mine. I give you my word that you won't be subjected to any further indignities. You must understand. The routine we put you through works both ways. It can prove a man innocent just as much as it can prove another guilty.'

'I suppose you were trying to prove me innocent when you put me in a three-legged chair under a locomotive headlight and had your menials accuse me of every crime in the calendar! What do you think I am?'

'I think,' the large man answered soberly, 'that you are a badly confused and thoroughly frightened man.'

'Thanks. When I want your help I'll call for it.'

'You won't have to call for it, sir. It shouldn't be necessary to remind you that it is neither for you or for me to say whether or not I'll work on your affairs now. If you are innocent, my work will prove it. I can assure you — '

'That you'll leave no stone unturned. I know. Where are you taking me?'

'You were fond of her. I thought you might like to see where she died.'

'Really? I was under the impression that you believed I had already seen it. At first hand.'

'I haven't said that, Mr. Elliot. I'm sorry you choose to be so sarcastic. I had thought that a man of your position and intelligence might know better than to permit his anger to get the best of him. If

193

you stopped a moment to consider, you might realize that I am just about the most important friend you've got right now.'

'I see. Perhaps I am beginning to understand. Your approach is considerably more ingenious than Mr. Axelrod's was. How much do you want?'

For a moment Dickerson's face went completely red. He seemed to swell. His nostrils flared and the pupils of his eyes went from grey to black. His large thick hands closed and opened again slowly.

And then, in a voice that was neither deep nor faintly musical, Dickerson said, 'If I thought you meant that, Mr. Elliot, I would make arrangements for you to be in even more trouble than you are now.'

They rode the rest of the way in silence. When they came at last to a debris-choked alley and Dickerson, in the lead, wordlessly pointed, Christopher was suddenly and violently sick.

★   ★   ★

Perhaps you could not blame him.

He could not work. He could not concentrate. Lines merged, converged, became blurred and were lost. Figures did not make sense, would not add, seemed unable to retain their normal sweeps and serifs. His hand held a pencil, but the hand refused the commands of his brain.

He could not sit, or stand with head bent down. He could not remain in any one spot. The walls of the room would fade and become dirty, soot-streaked brick. The furniture would turn to broken crates, battered cans and piles of refuse. The floor carpet would melt to mouldering garbage and the odour sifted up from his feet and threatened to strangle him.

He sent the rest of them away, Margaret and Griggs and Flanders. They knew something was wrong with him, something beyond the fact of his being in desperate trouble. They tendered him the respect of avoidance, but he could not permit them to remain and watch him disintegrate. So he sent them away.

When they had gone he locked the door and jammed a chair under the knob. He dragged a drawing-table over to supplement the chair, and the slight exertion left him giddy and panting. The air that he breathed held the sharpness of sandpaper in his lungs. The floor seemed hundreds of feet below him, the walls wavered, became obtuse, and the ceiling shimmered like a billowing tent.

With a little groan he fell to his knees and, swaying, fought to rise and then could fight no more.

How long he had slept, Christopher did not know. It was the telephone that roused him. He sat up, rubbing his neck and blinking his eyes. The lights of a theatre filtered in through the broad windows, and the flasher sign of the marquee made a rippling pattern on the wall.

Priming his dry mouth with a tongue that was no less dry he crawled until he gained the desk, reached up and pulled himself erect. His feet were numb and swollen, and he hobbled in an attempt to restore circulation. His groping hand encountered a light switch and more by accident than design he turned it on.

He swayed, blinking, and the telephone issued a longer sharper summons.

He reached the telephone and it was minutes before he could speak even thickly.

'Mr. Elliot?'

He knew that voice. It drove some of the fog from his brain. Stiffening he answered, 'So you already know where I am.'

'Your whereabouts is one secret you won't be able to keep from us for long, Mr. Elliot. I thought you'd be interested to learn that we've found Ruth Cassell's trunk.'

'What?' He wasn't asleep now. He gripped the telephone. 'Where did you find it?'

'Curious though the incident may have seemed, the explanation is quite logical. The owner of the house was driving past, saw the trunk and suspected his tenant might be getting ready to skip. He notified the renting agent and the agent beat the expressman by a matter of minutes.'

He exhaled slowly. The owner, Arthur Brokaw; the agent, Bill Donath — 'Thank you for calling, Lieutenant.'

'Not at all. Did you cut your hand while closing the trunk?'

'No. I had cut it on the glass of the kitchen door.' He stiffened. 'Why do you ask?'

'We found a smear on the hasp. Awkward things, those. You must have reopened the cut while closing the hasp. That would explain it.'

He took a long breath. 'Lieutenant, I've had a little sleep and things look different to me. I want to apologize for my actions this afternoon.'

'Thank you, Mr. Elliot. I realized that you were not yourself. If you have the chance tomorrow, stop in. We don't want to grill you, understand, but I'm sure you could help us.'

'I — I don't believe I should. Kaufman said — '

'Bring Kaufman along if you wish. We're having the devil's own job learning anything about the Cassell girl. I thought you could help us there.'

'I'm afraid I don't know very much about her. Have you any further line on Axelrod?'

'Nothing. He hasn't called on any of our monitored lines. I know you can help us there.'

'I? How can I? I haven't the faintest idea who the man is!'

'Perhaps not, Mr. Elliot, but you must certainly know who hired him. Think it over tonight and drop in tomorrow if it's convenient.'

Christopher replaced the telephone and thoughtful lines gathered in his forehead. He looked about and for the first time really saw the room. Since he needed a headquarters, some place from which to operate, this would do. Dickerson knew he was here, but Dickerson would know where he was anyway. He had no desire to go back to the club; he'd get a sleeping-room here in the hotel and have his bag sent over — no. Some eager newshound might be keeping tabs on that bag. Let it remain where it was.

He felt his jowls and discovered that already he needed to shave again. His eyes travelled to the door and he saw the barricade he had built. He grinned foolishly at it and then began replacing drawing board and chair. When he had finished he unlocked the door and opened it to glance cautiously into the hall. The hall, a *cul de sac*, was empty, but by the threshold was a small pile of mail.

Probably Margaret had brought it when she finished at the office. He'd have to caution her.

He returned to the desk. The mail consisted of four letters and a small package, all addressed to him at the office. He shuffled through the letters. There was one from Lyman Ashton and he opened it.

Sorry, old man . . . not much progress . . . perhaps if you saw her yourself . . . deeply shocked about the turn of affairs . . . there is anything I can do . . .

He tossed it aside impatiently.
One of the remainders was from his

club, probably containing a bill; he didn't bother with it. Next was a letter from Arthur Brokaw, offering sympathy and support, and he frowned speculatively at it before putting it aside.

On the last one the name and address were typed and the name was misspelled, a double 't' appearing at the end. He ran his thumb disinterestedly under the flap and drew out a letter written in ink on ruled paper.

He had read but a few words when he was staring incredulously.

Dear Sir, I have just read in the morning paper about the death of my daughter Ruth and that you are held as a 'material witness'. I am not sure what this means, but I know you were her friend because in one of the infrequent letters she wrote home she spoke of you and what a privilege it was to work with a man of your reputation.

I must say I am very shocked and aggrieved to have such bad news of her after hearing nothing for almost six months. She was my only child, I almost died with her, and after her father passed on we did not have things easy. Her stepfather and I slaved and almost starved to give her an education. She meant so much to us, so you see I cannot understand all that has happened so suddenly.

I have not written to the police because they would come here, and I do not want her stepfather to know. He is very sick with heart trouble and it would kill him if he knew, but could you find out if she had any insurance or savings as we are in desperate need of money.

Thanking you in advance for any help you can give, believe me, very sincerely and. humbly, Mrs. Ruth (Cassell) Hanscomb

P.S. I am giving this to a neighbour to address and mail as I cannot leave Mr. Hanscomb for long. R.H.

He dropped the letter and snatched at the envelope. The envelope was postmarked 'Tremont, 10 a.m.'

Tremont. A mill town, no more than

fifty or sixty miles to the north.

So here was the reason why Ruth Cassell had been uncommunicative about her past. She had been poor, dirt poor, and she had wanted no one to know it. He had thought her bored in the presence of the smart and sophisticated people at the Donaths; he had mistaken for ennui her wretchedness, a sense of inferiority and being misfit. No wonder she had been so receptive to him, so ripe and ready to lie in his arms —

Angrily he shook himself from the mood. He made his fingers busy, tearing first into particles and then into shreds the letter from her mother. He would get to her. He would beat the police. He would reach her before Dickerson did because there were things he had to know before Dickerson knew them.

But there were other things he had to do first.

He had been so absorbed in the letter he had almost forgotten the package. It was small and light, not over three inches square and about an inch deep. It had been addressed in neatly block-printed letters with pen and ink. There was no return address and the cancellation was an illegible smear.

His fingers struggled with the stout twine and then impatiently he grasped scissors. The paper wrapping, white, was evidently a letterhead that had been trimmed to size; it enclosed a plain grey box of the sort frequently used for costume jewellery.

When he lifted the cover and saw the dead mouse inside he nearly went insane.

7

Eddie Culbright bent down from his full five-feet-eight and opened parcel locker number twenty-four. Holding the door back with his leg he slid a heavy suitcase into the locker and followed it with a neat, square, patent-leather case. He remained for a minute, grinning at the luggage and liking the picture it made.

Then he closed the door, inserted a dime in the slot and, turning the handle, removed the key and placed it in his pocket. *The key is your receipt:* he filed that in a neat cubby-hole in his brain, and with it the position of the locker, bottom row, third from the left.

Straightening up, he said, 'Now we'll eat.'

She had been Mrs. Eddie Culbright for all of two days but she wasn't listening to him. She wasn't even looking at him. She had turned away and was gazing fixedly toward the waiting room.

'Eddie,' she whispered. 'That man — '

'What man? Where?'

'That man over there. The one who's trying to act as if we hadn't noticed — there! He just turned his head! I saw him out of the corner of my eye as we came past. He was watching us. While you were putting the bags in the locker he smiled at me and wrote something down on that pad he's trying to hide in his lap.'

'Oh, he *did*!' Eddie bristled. He knew all about railway stations and the kind of people who used them as headquarters for the Lord only knew what kind of goings-on. He swelled. He walked over to the benches, singled out the man and grunted, 'Hey, you!'

The worried-looking target of Eddie Culbright's attention did not seem immediately to realize that he was being addressed. He continued to watch the area of the parcel lockers with grim concentration. When Eddie's five-eight blocked his view he had to glance up. He looked doubtful at first, and then he indulged in a smile that made him appear even more like a horse than usual.

'Who, me?'

'Yes, you. What are you doing?'

'Oh, just checkin'.'

'Checking?'

'Yeah. You're blockin' my view — would you mind?'

Eddie hesitated only fractionally. He did an about-face and marched back to his bride. 'Come along,' he ordered, grasping her firmly by the arm.

Her high heels tappity-tapped on the stone floor. 'What — was — he — doing?'

'Oh, just checking. He had sort of a map there with squares on it. He was making marks on the squares. Probably works for a statistical organization. The stuff people want to know about these days!'

'Oh, Eddie,' she sighed and fell into step. 'You're so wonderful!'

★   ★   ★

Christopher dismissed the cab and stood facing his house. There was another car, he noticed, parked in the street beyond the driveway, but it looked empty and after briefly scanning it he turned his full attention to the house. It was only three days since he had left, and not yet two since Henrietta had taken the children and Agnes with her to the Geers, but already the house had on it the stamp of desertion.

He exhaled slowly and began climbing the driveway. The morning was sunny and warm but he shivered a little as he approached. He turned up the brick steps, crossed the level terrace and climbed two wide steps to the entrance. He was fitting key to lock when he heard a sound behind him.

Christopher turned and saw, standing between the rhododendrons that guarded the entrance to the breezeway, a stranger. Strange yet familiar. A vague type, the kind seen on buses and trains, on streets and in hallways; the type seen and never remembered.

'Mr. Elliot?'

Christopher stepped down from the landing. 'What do you want?'

The stranger moved swiftly. A camera suddenly blocked out his face and a flashbulb winked.

Christopher lunged forward, bellowing in anger. He held the advantages of counter-surprise and of not being encumbered. He caught the fellow as the camera was coming down, knocked it from his hands and spun him around with a jolting blow to the shoulder. He jumped, landed his heel squarely on the camera and then kicked the wreckage along the terrace.

'Get out!' he shouted.

The fellow acted dazed. Not angry or frightened, but as if he could not quite comprehend what had happened to him or his camera. Watching Christopher, he stooped down and groped until he found his hat. It was old, and in the force of its fall the band had come off and was suspended by a thread, but he did not notice as he put it on. Still watching Christopher he sidled across the terrace until he reached his camera. He picked it up and his glance wavered and fell to the collapsed remains.

'You swine!' His eyes crystallized sharply.

'Mike!'

A new voice, shouting, from an owner unseen.

'Come on, Mike! Let's get the hell out of here!'

Christopher glared uncertainly about, trying to locate the source of the voice. He found it, almost simultaneously with his discovery of the unnatural movement of the clump of evergreens bordering the drive.

He could not move in two directions at once, and his indecision cost him both. When he was halfway to the evergreens he heard a car door slam and an engine leap to instant, roaring life. When he had turned, the fellow called Mike was in the driveway and running like a deer for the street.

Christopher vented his rage in an angry shrug and a scowl. At least he'd smashed their camera for them. That would show them. They might be able to bulldoze and browbeat some people, but they would learn to leave Christopher Elliot alone.

In his anger he almost forgot why he was here. He would have gone back to the street and walked to the centre of town if belated memory had not held him. He turned and entered the house.

★ ★ ★

He did not stay long. What he had thought an empty house could give him he did not know, and he was sorry he had come. His brief inspection told him that Henrietta and the children had moved out completely, probably never to return.

After that he remained only long enough to learn, via telephone, that Bill Donath was in his office and could spare him a few minutes.

★ ★ ★

Bill was busy with a client when Christopher came in. Bill's secretary favoured Christopher with a long, uncensored glance, showed him to a chair, got him a magazine, lingered and then departed in a huff when he glared at her.

He had no stomach for the magazine and so he took the opportunity to study Bill. The last time he'd seen him, Bill was a collapsed alcoholic heap, spread out on a bed. Now, while his face was pinched and pasty and there was a certain vagueness about his eyes, the whites of his eyes were clear and both his movements and evident attention showed that he had himself under control. An open box of candy was on the desk and as Christopher watched, Bill took a chocolate from it and ate it.

The client sat facing away from Christopher and several times he acted as if he might be getting ready to leave. Finally they did reach an end. The client stood, turned halfway around and Christopher recognized him as the proprietor of a local department store. Bill got up, crossed to another room, and when he reappeared was wearing topcoat and hat.

Christopher arose in dismay. As they came by him he said, 'I wanted to see you, Bill. It's quite important and I haven't much time.'

'Well — ' Donath hesitated, glancing helplessly at his client. 'You know each other, don't you?'

'Of course,' Forbes indulged in a

fawning smile. 'I used to meet Mr. Elliot on the golf course occasionally. How are you, sir?'

Forbes wouldn't mention the store. Nor, evidently, did he choose to indicate that he had met Christopher much more recently in the columns of his newspaper.

Bill said, 'We were going up to my place. Forbes is looking for a house, and I'm thinking seriously about selling mine. Might as well. I don't have any need for it now.'

Forbes chuckled. 'Yes. Why not ride along with us? Maybe you could keep this super-salesman off my neck while I look around on my own and get some idea of what the place is worth.'

★   ★   ★

It was half an hour before they had a minute alone. Forbes had progressed to the yard and was critically examining garden and shrubs. They were in the kitchen, watching from the mullion windows above the sink.

'It's a rum go,' Christopher said,

213

sensing Bill's distaste.

'You ought to know.' Bill brought himself back from a distant line of thought. 'What about this mess you're in? Are you in the clear?'

'I don't know. I didn't kill her, if that's what you mean.'

'Ruth Cassell,' Bill sighed and shook his head. 'It doesn't seem possible. She was one of my wife's — one of Marge's friends at school. You know how Marge was. Always kind to stray animals. I guess Ruth didn't have many friends. And to think you met her in this house!'

Now. He's made the break himself. Now is the time. 'Was Ruth the — the girl you were involved with?'

Bill's fishlike eyes held bewilderment. 'Was Ruth *what*?'

'The girl. The one who broke up your home. The reason Marge left you.'

'Ruth Cassell?' Vagueness crystallized to shock. 'Don't be absurd, Chris! Do you mean to tell me that all the stuff in the papers was true? I mean, about her being your mistress? Ruth didn't impress me as that sort of girl at all. Imagine them printing stuff like that!'

'Bill, who was the woman? You never told me.'

Bill's face and eyes became thoughtful, wary. Soberly he said, 'I'd rather not tell you. It isn't that it's a point of honour or something, but if you don't mind I'd rather not.'

'Look, Bill.' Christopher faced him squarely. He was ominously calm. 'We're in the same boat. Henrietta left me. We're in the same boat except that I'm under suspicion of murder, and besides I have two kids. You and I have been closer than friends; your father was my partner. Now that we're both in trouble, the least you can do is play square with me. I want to know the woman's name.'

'So, you really think it *was* Ruth Cassell.' Bill flushed to the roots of his thinning hair. 'Can't you understand? You knew me pretty well. You knew I never fooled with women. Doesn't it mean anything to you that no one, even the filthy rotten newspapers with all their digging, could find out who the woman was, or even if there was a woman?' Bill turned away and his voice became bitter. 'You say you're my friend. Won't you let me keep what little of my self-respect I have?'

Christopher looked at the cringing figure and the anger drained from him. Suddenly he understood. There had been no woman. The woman had been invented for the sake of Bill's mother and for a society that might wink when a man got himself messed up with a tramp, but was horrified when he took seriously to the bottle.

There was no 'other woman'. Marge had left him because he couldn't stop drinking.

Dead end.

They stood elbow to elbow, leaning against the sink, each occupied by his separate thoughts. They were standing thus when Forbes came stamping in from the yard.

'Well,' Forbes announced, 'frankly I like your place. Well-built, nicely arranged, good location. Good neighbourhood. Neighbourhood counts these days. You

216

never know what you're apt to find next door to you.'

Christopher moved away from them. One of his big ideas had failed; just why he had thought it so big he was now unable to fathom. He had met Ruth here; Ruth had rented the cottage through Bill; Bill's office had seized her trunk — it had seemed logical enough when pieced together that way, but in the long run what did it amount to?

'No, I won't want the furniture,' Forbes was saying. 'Got too much of my own. There's one thing, though, I wouldn't mind owning. Your record player and recorder. It sure is a beauty — '

The recorder. The thing you talked or sang or whistled into, and it would talk and sing and whistle back to you. The same thing over and over again, as many times as you wished, whenever you wanted it to —

Whenever you wanted it to!

He interrupted them. He confused hell out of poor Bill and almost scared Forbes out of his wits. He was talking much too fast at first, and it required tremendous effort to make his question clear.

'Record blanks?' Bill regarded him with bewilderment. 'I don't know, Chris. I think I bought six. Yes, I'm sure it was six. They were so much a dozen, and I didn't want a whole dozen. But my God, I don't remember how many we used. Maybe two or three. They're in the record cabinet. You can count them if it's that important.

He did not wait for the puzzled glances he knew must be passing between them; already he was running for the living room. When he reached the cabinet he dropped on his knees and flung open the doors. Recklessly he spilled records out on to the rug and went pawing through them.

Round metal discs, eight inches in diameter. He found one, and then almost immediately another, and that was all in this lot. He attacked the cabinet, pulling out more records, and so found a third and fourth. Then he pulled out albums, covers, everything until the cabinet was completely bare.

He found the fifth of the round metal

discs inside a Brunswick album of jazz classics.

Bill Donath and the man Forbes stood at a distance, watching him. They appeared to be too surprised to speak, too stunned to move.

They acted as if they were a little afraid of him.

He collected all the discs he had found and set them carefully aside. Once more he searched the remaining pile, turning them one by one with the greatest care. When he was done and no more of the discs had appeared he sighed, a shuddering escape of breath.

He got to his feet. 'Five,' he said, and held them out. 'You bought six, you now have five. You wouldn't have been likely to break any because they're metal. Did you give one to anybody?'

Bill shook his head. 'We didn't give any away. All six of them should be there. What does it mean? What are you trying to prove?'

Christopher exhaled slowly. 'It means that I heard what I heard. It means that I'm no more insane than you are. Who's been in here? Who's used this recorder? Did you give anyone permission to use it?'

'I don't know, Chris. Lots of people have been in here. You know that. I don't recall giving anyone express permission to use the recorder. What's wrong? Tell me what you're trying to prove.'

He did not answer. Suddenly he did not trust them.

He left them standing there, their glances shifting from him to the spilled records and then to each other.

⋆ ⋆ ⋆

So the cat's cry, then, had been relayed over the telephone from a phonograph record. It was so simple, so logical that he was utterly convinced. And he was further convinced that the record had been made on the machine in Bill Donath's house, and that the record in fact was the missing metal disc. It would have been easy for anyone who knew of such a machine; a cinch for anyone to slip into Bill's house and make an impromptu sound studio of his living room. Bill had been on a bender for more than a week prior to the first broadcast of the crying cat. And Bill, even when sober, seldom locked his house.

The torturer of the cat had possessed a full week's time in which to accomplish a few minutes' work.

Who knew that he had such a recorder? Everyone who knew him. Everyone who had been to his house within the past eight months. That would include Cissie Folwell, Lyman Ashton, Arthur Brokaw and his wife. And Wick. And Henrietta.

Who of these people would be capable of such a thing? Cissie Folwell? Eminently. But, why? Lyman Ashton? Probably. But again, why? Arthur or Lambie Pie? No. There wasn't the imagination in the pair of them to conceive such an idea. But, Wick?

Wick was capable. Wick had had opportunity. Wick had been sitting there half the night, waiting. Wick could have hired the detective or whatever it was the unknown Axelrod had represented himself to be. Wick would have been only too happy to present Henrietta with evidence of Christopher's philandering. In his mind's eye he could see Wick planning Henrietta's train trip to Reno, poring over timetables, setting down a schedule; he would be sure to caution her about turning the clock back as she entered each new time zone; he would warn her about speaking to strangers on the train.

Wick would have loved that.

Christopher's face was a tight mask as he left the corner by Bill Donath's house and turned into Crescent Street. It was little more than a block to the Geer house and he wanted to go there first because he wanted to see Henrietta. He wanted to see her in Wick's presence and while he watched Wick's face tell her of the discovery he'd made.

He was within a hundred yards of the Geer house when he saw a group on the steps. He spotted the blue of a policeman's uniform and sudden fear clutched at his heart. His steps quickened. But when he had come near enough to catch details he stopped.

One of those on the steps was the

photographer named Mike. With him was another man and the policeman. They had Wick cornered on the porch. For once Wick was displaying some emotion. He was waving his arms.

'I tell you that none of the Elliot family is here!'

That much Christopher heard in Wick's high-pitched excited voice.

Swiftly he turned into a driveway and passed behind a house to avoid being seen. He crossed behind another house, covered a broad stretch of lawn and came into Crescent Street. He turned away from the centre of town and began climbing the long sloping hill.

If Henrietta was not at the Geers', there was only one other place she could be.

★   ★   ★

The Folwell mansion was a pseudo-Georgian affair with a great expanse of pillars, dormer windows, slate roof and whitewashed brick walls. It was massive, impressive and no doubt deeply satisfying to a man who had mixed his first supply of patent medicine in a tub in the basement of a Chelmere farmhouse; but as an architectural accomplishment it hadn't quite come off.

Unpleasant though the house might be, the grounds surrounding it were beautifully landscaped and scrupulously kept up. The grounds were protected by a whitewashed brick wall that — all Chelmere knew because Frank Folwell had boasted of it — contained a million bricks and was over two miles long. The building of the wall had been Folwell's contribution to the local relief situation, but the motive was obscure. Perhaps he had not been so much moved by a desire to alleviate poverty as he had been to protect himself from it.

The wall was fittingly equipped with gates of wrought iron and a postern lodge. There was a pull-cord by the gate and Christopher gave it a tug.

The door of the lodge opened and a wizened, bent old man came shuffling out.

'Hello, Amos! How are you? How is the rheumatism?'

The old man stopped, a dozen feet from the inside of the gate. His face was shrivelled and shrunken as a monkey's, and the eyes that inspected Christopher were dim and rheumy.

'It's all right. It's only me.' He lifted his hat.

The indecision of the aged was on the gate's guardian; the hesitant, apologetic, patient waiting. He stood and made no move to come nearer the gate.

'Amos! It's me, Christopher Elliot! You know me. I want to see my wife and Mrs. Folwell!'

The old man slowly turned and began shuffling back to the lodge.

'Amos!' Christopher seized the upright bars. 'Have you lost your mind? Damn you, let me in!' Fury swelled within him. He tried with all his strength to shake the gate, to move it, to make it yield. He might as well have attacked the wall.

The door of the lodge closed on the old man's back.

Christopher recoiled as if struck in the

face. So that was how things stood. Amos had his orders. Mr. Elliot was not to be admitted under any circumstances. This place becomes a fortress to Mr. Elliot, and you and your gate are the first line of defence. Mr. Elliot is an undesirable, a madman.

Keep him out.

He began to walk beside the wall. His brain was working at top speed, seeking ahead, searching the wall, probing its weaknesses. It ran neither straight nor level; the further he went the more uneven the ground became. He passed from a field into an orchard. Great piles of prunings lay about on the ground, and against the wall in many places were the blackened scars of long-dead bonfires.

That showed what this honest farmer thought of Frank Folwell's wall.

Christopher paused for breath, looked about him, and then his heart began to pound exultantly. Less than a few feet away, leaning against the bole of a stately old apple tree, was a ladder.

The ladder was light and appeared to be strong, and when he had carried it a little way he found a rise of ground, an outcropping of ledge against the wall. Carefully he set the ladder upright, leaned it against the wall and stepped back.

The shafts extended above the top.

He climbed swiftly and as his head cleared the wall he paused in study, trying to adjust his perspective and recall just where he would be when he landed within. Ahead of him, through the branches of trees, he saw enough of roof and siding to recognize the garage.

He finished his climb, threw his feet up and lay flat on his stomach, panting, on the broad top of the wall. Behind him the ladder wavered, slid sideways and fell to the ground. He was powerless to stop it.

He waited, resting, breathing deeply, thinking and planning. He would go straight to the garage, around it and into the house by the service entrance. Once inside no one could stop him from seeing Henrietta and the children. And no one would stop him from reaching the house. The children might not understand, but

Henrietta would, after he was finished —

He inched around, let his feet down on the inside, lay on his stomach a moment, let himself down until he was hanging by his hands, closed his eyes, gave a violent outward kick and let go.

He landed in soft loam. The ground sloped rapidly from the wall and his momentum carried him down in a reverse somersault. He came to rest face downward and he lay, waiting for sensation to tell him if the fall had been bad.

There was no pain beyond the numbness of shock. His arm ached, and there was a twinge in the knee that had struck the wall too sharply. But there was no sensation of sprain or fracture.

He sat up, recovered his hat, brushed dirt from it, punched it into shape and put it on. He got to his feet and limped a few cautious, testing steps. Then he headed for the garage.

Christopher had gained the garage and was peering about at the macadam parking space when a blow grazed his ear and nearly knocked him down.

With the swiftness of a camera-shutter Christopher's eye caught and recorded even the minutest details. His hulking attacker had a mole at the side of his misshapen nose. His bloodshot eyes were small and stupid. One of his ears was permanently closed. Fat folded from his neck over his collar. His hatless close-cropped head was flecked with grey.

Christopher rolled aside, slid along the garage wall, and came back with fists flailing.

Even as he began he knew that the balance was tipped against him. He was hampered by the topcoat. He could give neither drive nor distance to his first. His right arm was heavy and disobedient. Blows that should have landed solidly fell short and he was floundering.

It was over quickly.

★ ★ ★

He was lying on the sands at Miami Beach. The sun was pouring down relentlessly. The others around him were huddled beneath umbrellas, seeking the little relief of shade, but he was unprotected and he was cool. The sands were cool and the sun was cool and the ocean that washed up and around him was black as night and dry as air. He moved his head and let the air-black ocean caress his cheeks.

A small pain began to grow in the middle of his back. It was probably caused by a stone or a shell in the sand. He would have moved, rolling over away from it, had he not been so comfortable.

The pain grew.

He decided to roll over, and he discovered he could not move. His brain told his hands to push down and his body to turn, but he saw the message travel down his arms and his body until it reached fingers and toes and then left him to sink, protesting, into the black sands.

He was terrified and helpless when the sun noticed him and left the heavens to come down. The sun's face was terribly hot at first and it burned through his eyeballs into his brain and on through the back of his head. And then his brain cooled and he dared open his eyes and he saw that the sun's face was old and wrinkled and kindly; beautiful white hair curled about his temples and his faded blue eyes were deep with concern.

'I ... can't ... move,' Christopher gasped and suddenly he was no longer anywhere but in a ditch outside the Folwell wall.

'I shouldn't wonder!' The head that had been bent above him straightened and the old eyes looked anxiously up and down the road. Christopher recognized him then as the farmer neighbour of the Folwells, the one who owned the fruit trees.

The farmer left him and strode to the gate. Righteously angry, he resembled Job as he shouted at the postern lodge and all that it represented.

'There's a man out here that's been bad hurt! Looks like a hit and run. If you people won't take him in you can at least give me a hand so's I can get him into my truck!'

The walls and the lodge gave back

nothing save silence.

Job hurriedly left off his siege when he saw that Christopher was sitting up. He came running, his gnarled hands offering support.

'I think I can manage,' Christopher said thickly. 'It — it seems to be mostly in my back.'

'I shouldn't wonder. You landed on a sharp rock there. Your back might be broke. Think you ought to try?'

Christopher did not answer. Against the farmer's objections he staggered to his feet and, disdaining assistance, made it to the truck.

★   ★   ★

He awoke to the pounding insistence that time was slipping away. He started to sit up, winced with pain and dropped back groaning to the pillow.

His whole body throbbed like an abscessed tooth. The pain was general, but there were sharper localities of it. With increasing consciousness the pain drained from the network of his body into

232

separate deepening pools. From the point of his jaw to the base of his skull. His right forearm from elbow to wrist. From sternum to spine, between his lungs. His right knee and his right ankle.

For the moment he forgot where he had been and what had happened to him. He tried to recall where he was.

Sunlight streamed in the window, filling the small room until it seemed that its walls must burst or the furniture collapse from the pressure. His eyes accustomed themselves to the light and brought recognition. He was in the Hotel Paulson. To his left, no more than eight feet away, was a bathroom with a reward, if he could reach it, of a waiting hot shower.

His head rolled to the left and he saw his valise and he remembered more.

He had picked up the valise at his house in Chelmere. He had ridden to the house in a truck driven by a farmer. The farmer had wanted to take him either to a hospital or the police station. The farmer had insisted that he had been struck by a car on the road in front of the Folwell estate.

When Christopher remembered the Folwell wall he got up, despite his pain, and lurched to the bathroom. He pushed himself along the wall until his groping hands found the shower faucets, and turning both on full he thrust his head in the drenching torrent.

★　★　★

The glass-panelled door of Dickerson's office opened discreetly and Connelly's long face peered through. Connelly's eyes made a hasty survey and then the rest of him whisked in. He made straight for the desk and worry was on his face from one lopsided ear to the other.

'How much longer you want us to keep that set-up at the station, Chief?'

Dickerson had been frowning at the front page account, complete with three-column picture, of Christopher Elliot's altercation with a cameraman. Mr. Elliot, evidently, had not realized another photographer was hidden in his evergreens.

'He has a bad temper, that one,'

234

Dickerson shook his head reprovingly. His glance travelled up from the paper. 'What did you ask me?'

'How much longer are we gonna waste time watchin' those parcel lockers at the railroad station? You know the baggage master has 'em checked every twenty-four hours, and if the meter hasn't changed they pull the lock and take the contents to the baggage room.'

'I am aware of that.' Dickerson's face was slightly pink. 'It is also possible that you and I are not the only people who are aware of it.'

'Natch. But I don't get it, Chief. Even assumin' your hunch is right an' the killer might've stashed somethin' in one of those lockers, we should've had it by now. Today's Friday. She was killed Tuesday night. If anything was put in a locker Tuesday night, the lock would've been pulled yesterday mornin'. And even if the checker might've missed yesterday, he wouldn't've missed again this mornin'. So what?'

Dickerson sighed. 'What were my instructions?'

'First, we were to see if anyone come in there and put in another dime without takin' anything out.'

'Right. Did anyone do that?'

'No.'

'And then?'

'Check with the baggage master to see if any stuff was pulled out and sent to the baggage room for extra charges.'

'Correct. Have we done that?'

'Poz. No business.'

'My hunch could be wrong,' Dickerson admitted. 'But we've searched that whole area with a fine-tooth comb and we haven't turned up the pistol or anything else. Regardless, there was a pistol, and from the alley where Ruth Cassell was killed to the railway terminal the distance is less than two blocks.'

Connelly's face mirrored anguish. 'But, Chief — '

'I know. It doesn't make sense. I could be wrong. Maybe the killer is toting a hot rod around in his pocket. Or maybe he hid it in the flush-tank of a johnny somewhere, or he might have chartered a plane and dropped it in the middle of the ocean. Maybe we're not looking for a pistol. I don't know. I do know that our set-up has proved one thing.'

'That there's nothin' in those lockers!'

'No. It's proved that if there *is* anything, the person was smart enough not to lock it up and take away the key.'

'*That* don't make any sense.'

'I disagree. When you want to hide something, one of the best methods is not to hide it at all. Suppose you wanted to ditch a pistol; if you put it in a parcel locker, inserted a dime and took the key with you, within forty-eight hours at most the pistol would be discovered. You could delay it by returning to the locker once each day and inserting a new dime, but in that case our set-up would catch you.

'But if, instead of going to all that trouble, you merely threw the pistol all the way to the back of a locker, especially one of those in the bottom row, someone else would come along, deposit a suitcase in front of it, pay the dime for you, take the key away and your secret would be safe. You would be safe until either the renter or a subsequent renter overstayed his time or if, at inspection, the locker happened to be empty and the baggage master took the trouble to examine it.'

'Yeah? Why wouldn't the first guy to put somethin' in the locker see it and report it?'

'He might, but the further the locker is from eye level, the less the chance. Those lockers are in constant use. Many times a fresh renter is right on the heels of the previous one. He is primarily concerned with getting his baggage in the locker; after it's in is when he inspects, if at all. Think back and recall, if you can, how many objects you've found in supposedly empty lockers; the score is probably none. Yet go to the baggage room and see the number of galoshes, rubbers, umbrellas, packages and heaven knows what are turned up every morning.'

Connelly stared. 'Well, I'll be go to hell,' he said.

'We'll keep the set-up another twenty-four hours. If nothing's turned up by tomorrow morning we'll have the baggage master pull all the locks, starting with the bottom rows. After that you may call me anything you wish.'

The door opened and McGhee came briskly in. She handed a typescript to Dickerson and said, 'Doctor Pfeifer sent this, Lieutenant. It's the analysis you wanted.' Turning, she went briskly out.

Dickerson read slowly, aloud, 'Substance on labia determined to be graphite; largely carbon, wax and lampblack with presence of some clay and silicates noted. Either Mitchell or Locard tests impractical due to negligible quantity.'

'What,' Connelly demanded, 'does that word 'labia' mean?'

'The lips, you knucklehead, the lips.' Dickerson began pawing amongst the papers on his desk, finally found the one he wanted and read again, slowly and aloud:

'Contents of pockets: nothing. Contents of purse: twenty-five cents coin; Tangee lipstick; gold compact; two handkerchiefs; benzedrine inhaler; common doorkey; Central Railway timetable; two Yale and cabinet keys on ring in leather container; unused portion (five trips) of ten-trip railway ticket to Chelmere; duplicate sales slip Madame Renault's shop, Grant Avenue; two sticks gum; half-package lemon drops; rubber band; Parker fountain pen.'

'The stuff,' Connelly grunted, 'that dames lug around.'

'Yes, and what's more to the point, the stuff they *don't* lug around. Do you see a pencil anywhere in that list?'

'Pencil?' Connelly looked again. 'Nope.'

Dickerson stood up. He was chewing vigorously on his moustache. Abruptly he asked, 'Do you know if they've picked up Malloy yet?'

'Malloy? Who Malloy? You mean that private dick?'

'I mean Bud Malloy and no one else. Find out if Farlane got him yet, and if he has, see if you can pick up Christopher Elliot.'

8

Slowly he came up the narrow, cluttered street. He was limping a little, although for the most part he walked steadily enough. Had you not known him you would have noticed nothing wrong unless you were close enough to see the angry welt on his jaw and the puffy discoloration over his right eye.

As he walked further up the street he neared a scattered group of boys. The boys were playing one o' cat and the youth at bat was both noticing him and measuring the cat with practiced eye. When he came by a telephone pole the youth with the stick neatly tipped the end of the cat and with an experienced swing knocked it over Christopher's head.

The other boys set up a chorus of cries and swept around Christopher and beyond him, and the youth with the stick grinned and jogged unhurriedly to the telephone pole.

'Which house is the Hanscombs'?' Christopher asked, scowling.

The youth spat in the dust of the street and pointed with a thumb. 'Second one. The yellow one — ' He turned and sprinted for home base as one of the boys came charging back with the cat.

Christopher reached the yellow house, opened a slatternly gate and slowly climbed sagging steps. He gave the doorbell a twist. A diamond-shaped panel of glass was set in the door and when through it he saw a woman enter the hall, he removed his hat.

She opened the door and stood, looking at him out of eyes that were Ruth's, only older and more tired. She was pitifully thin and at the base of her throat was the beginning or the remains of a goiter. Her worn hands fumbled with her apron.

'You're Mr. Elliot,' she said finally.

'Yes. And you are Ruth's mother.'

She looked away. 'I can't ask you in. He doesn't know about it yet. He wouldn't understand why you were here.'

'That's all right, Mrs. Hanscomb. I'll not stay long.'

Her straying eyes returned to his and were a bit sharper. 'I've found out what 'material witness' means, Mr. Elliot.'

'If you hadn't, I would have told you anyway. Then you must know the police suspect me.'

'Yes.'

'I didn't, Mrs. Hanscomb.'

Her eyes held a moment, wavered and fell. 'I'm glad,' she responded simply. 'Glad for your sake. It doesn't make much difference to me who killed her. She's dead.'

'I want you to know that there were things about Ruth and me in the newspaper accounts, things which were totally untrue. She was a fine girl, one of the finest I've ever known.'

The woman looked at her worn hands. Her head nodded but she did not speak.

'Mrs. Hanscomb, was Ruth ever engaged to be married? Was there some boy here in Tremont, or after she left here, who was in love with her? Anyone who might have felt deeply enough about her to — to do this awful thing?'

The woman glanced up quickly, 'Oh, no, Mr. Elliot. Ruth never went out with boys, even when she was in high school. We had it pretty hard. I did work by the day, and when Ruth wasn't in school she was busy keeping house for her stepfather and me. She hated boys because they used to poke fun at her on account of her clothes. She always had to wear made-over dresses and her stockings were darned and her shoes were usually worn through. She hated the boys and the other girls and she wanted to make good so she could show them up. That's why she worked so hard. She got ahead better in school than the other girls and boys, so they resented her. She didn't have any friends at all.'

'But there must have been someone. When she was in college — she must have had some friends there. She went to a co-educational institution. She was a beautiful girl. There would have been someone. In her letters didn't she mention a particular boy, someone who might have wanted to take her out to parties or dances?'

The woman closed her eyes. Silence settled between them and even the sounds of the boys playing in the street and the hum of life in the town were distant, unrelated things. The woman moved her head slowly from side to side as if scanning in memory the pages written in a clear and beautiful script. Back, over the years, the pages falling like dead leaves —

'There was a man.' Her eyes opened, focused to noticeable sharpness. 'It was in Ruth's junior year. She worked summers, waiting on table in a hotel up at Brentwood Lakes, earning money for her clothing and expenses. She had a scholarship, but it was only enough to pay her books and tuition. She met a man at the hotel. She wrote home and said at last there was a man who acted like he might want to marry her. But she didn't like him. She said he was too old and too ugly. She told him to stop annoying her, and that's the last I heard of it.'

'His name! What was his name?'

The woman shook her head. 'Ruth never told me. She did say, though, that he was somebody important. Seems to me he was giving lectures at the hotel. He was only supposed to be there for a few days, but he stayed on for quite a spell. But she wouldn't have anything of him because he was too old.'

'Lectures — do you recall if Ruth said what he was lecturing about?'

'She didn't say, Mr. Elliot. She treated the whole thing as more or less of a joke.'

'I don't suppose she — ' Christopher paused in frowning thought. Abruptly he exhaled and shrugged his shoulders. 'I haven't yet been able to find out if Ruth had a savings account or life insurance. The police won't tell me anything. But if she did have them — ' He broke off and his eyes narrowed. 'Have the police been here?'

'Yes. A Mr. Dickerson was here yesterday afternoon.'

'Dickerson! What did he want?'

'He asked me questions mostly about — about you, Mr. Elliot. He said he'd searched her apartment, but he hadn't found any insurance policies or bank books, he said.'

Of course Dickerson wouldn't miss a chance to ask about him. Christopher was thoughtful as he reached in his pocket and produced a flat white envelope. 'I saw Mr. Landon, Ruth's employer. She had two weeks' vacation with pay plus a bonus coming to her. You'll find two hundred and fifty dollars here, and if you need any more I'll be glad to help.'

The woman accepted the envelope. She held it in her worn hands. Clutching it to her thin bosom she leaned against the doorjamb and began to weep softly.

★   ★   ★

The man was scrawny and old, and as he came to the front of his shop a pair of wirehaired fox terriers set up excited barking. In another wire enclosure a toy bull began to yap, and a bright green parrot in a brass cage cried, 'Shut up, you bloody little ra-a-t, shut up — awrk!'

'Yes, sir, what can I do for you?'

'Mice, white mice. Do you sell any white mice?'

'Sorry, I'm a little hard of hearing. You'll have to speak louder — ' He turned and glared at the parrot. 'Shut up, Mike! Now, mister, what was it you said?'

'Do you sell any *white mice?*' Christopher gave that line up as hopeless. Bringing envelope and pencil from his pocket he wrote swiftly: *Have you sold any white mice within the past month?*

The scrawny proprietor went to the front of the store where the light was better. He brought the envelope to within a foot of his nose and as he read he formed the words with his lips. Then he shook his head.

'We don't have any mice. Nobody wants 'em any more. The kids used to buy 'em, but the parents would give us hell for sellin' 'em. I lost a fifty-dollar-dog sale a year ago last Easter because I sold a twenty-five cent mouse to a kid on Westborne Terrace. His mother come in here and threw the mouse the whole length of the store.' He handed the envelope back to Christopher and memory made him angry. 'You're the second one's been in here about mice. The other was a cop. You'd think the cops had enough to do solvin' crimes without goin' around takin' up people's time — '

★ ★ ★

There were four pet shops on Ward Avenue, two on Grant and three on connecting side streets, and Christopher covered them all. There might have been more, but if so no one seemed to know anything about them. He picked up information about additional stores as he went along and finally he reached an end. There was no one who either had mice to sell or had sold any within a period ranging from six months to more than a year.

He did find men who expressed interest and a desire to co-operate. One solemn dealer recognized him from his newspaper pictures. This person treated Christopher as if he were a long-lost brother; in no time and without urging he confided that he too had been unjustly accused of murder some five years previously. He had been acquitted, but the attendant publicity had cost him his position and reduced him to this means of making a living. He quoted scripture and told Christopher to be brave and trust in God. He followed Christopher to the pavement and might have accompanied him on his search had there been some slight encouragement. Christopher hailed a cab and left his newfound friend waving goodbye as if the kerb were a pier and the cab a departing liner.

There were others, less sympathetic, but more practical. The essence of their suggestions was that he try hospitals, laboratories and the zoo.

He was near the Professional Building when he remembered Swinburne, and so he went up.

The leathery little pathologist was busy but whatever it was, he dropped it immediately. 'I've been reading your case in the newspapers,' he said. 'I had no idea, when you first came to me, how important the matter was. As a result I'm having my new girl make a complete search of the files. Naturally she can't work at it all the time, but she's managed to cover a lot of ground. We haven't found it yet, but we will.'

'Thank you. I'll pay for the girl's time. I — people are beginning to humour me, and sometimes I've wondered if there really ever was a mouse.'

'I understand how you must feel. There was a mouse, all right. The police have it now, and they're as interested as you are in finding out who it was that brought the previous mouse to me. Don't worry about charges. Frankly, the damned thing is so intriguing I take an occasional hand in the search myself.'

*   *   *

He came by a pit of buzzing serpents (the brass plate on the protecting glass said *Sistrurua miliarius:* Pygmy Rattlesnake, U.S.A.) and stopped to watch, fascinated, at the next cage as a fat, uniformed attendant opened a trap and dropped a squirming white rabbit inside. There was

251

no corner of the cage not containing a curved, arm-thick coil and the rabbit crouched, panting in fear. The coil moved slowly, lazily, scraping against the glass.

'Try to get out of that, you little swine,' the attendant chuckled. 'Got away from me once today, didn't you? Made me chase you all over the damned place. Go ahead, run! Get away from him. Tire him out. It's all right by me. I don't give a damn what you do now.'

Christopher shook off his fascination. 'You raise mice, too, don't you?'

'Sure. That's what we feed the big boy's little cousins in the next pit. They got rabbit ideas, but they have to eat mice.'

'Do you ever give any of your mice away, or sell them to the public?'

'Give 'em away? Hell, no! You ought to see some of these swine eat. The snakes are bad enough, but we got ocelots and coatis — ' He broke off. He had returned to watching the rabbit, and he said, 'Uhuh. Got you, hasn't he? You'll be with your brother in a minute.'

He stepped down. His manner changed perceptibly. 'You a doctor?' he asked.

'No. I'm interested in mice. Would it be possible for anyone to steal any mice from you?'

'Steal? Why would anybody want to steal a mouse? Most people want to get rid of 'em.'

'I don't mean that kind. I mean the white ones. I'm trying to find out if anyone could get to the place where the mice are kept.'

The attendant's manner changed again. 'No, Mack. Nobody can get to the mice. They're safe. We keep 'em in a nice white room, and nobody can get near 'em except me. If you want to see the mice, Mack, you'll have to come back in January. It's mating season now.'

A flush pounded to Christopher's temples. He clenched his hands, stood glaring a moment, and then turned on his heel and walked back the way he had come.

★　★　★

Dusk found him again in the centre of the city. He did not want to admit defeat, but he knew that the afternoon had been wasted. It had seemed so logical, so easy. There had been three white mice. The mice had come from somewhere. All he had to do, he had thought, was to visit places where mice were sold and find out who had bought them. If not names, then descriptions or anything tangible he could track down.

He was nearing the end now; he knew it. He could feel the end's approach, could sense a lifting of the fog and discern a shape in the mist.

Little as it was, he had come a long way for even this.

In the beginning there had been nothing. Only manifestations which at times had made him think he might be losing his mind. A woman, fleeing in the night. Running away — from what? He hadn't believed her. He'd thought the story of the cat on the telephone a fantastic thing, a scheme for sympathy or the imaginings of an unbalanced mind.

That was before he'd heard it himself.

He had seen the first mouse. Had seen

and held it in his hand and finally disposed of it. But instead of believing he had been annoyed. Had humoured her, really, in asking questions the while he thought she should see a psychiatrist.

Now they were beginning to humour him.

It should have been easy. The unseen could procure mice at will. Could deliver them by hand or send them by post, a cardboard box for a coffin and tissue paper for a shroud. He, after miles and hours of walking, riding, questioning and searching could not buy nor borrow nor steal one.

So then, the unseen hand of the discernible shape. The problem that in the beginning had been Ruth Cassell's was now, by inheritance or continuation, his alone.

One hope remained.

He quickened his steps and came at length to the business offices of the morning newspaper. Entering he went directly to the advertising department and there told the first person he saw exactly what he wanted.

He was on his way out of the building when he ran into Dickerson.

★ ★ ★

Dickerson gave the cab driver an address, settled back and turned a cold, searching glance on Christopher. His grey eyes appraised the discoloration above the eye and the welt on the chin.

Dickerson said, 'I've been trying all day to get in touch with you. Have you seen Kaufman? He's been trying too.'

'I've been busy.' Christopher thought it unnecessary to explain.

'Give it up, Elliot. It's no good.'

He flushed. 'I don't believe I understand you.'

'Your investigation. You're wasting time, duplicating our efforts, neglecting your business, getting nowhere, angering Kaufman, and you might be getting yourself into trouble.'

'Are you implying that I'm not in trouble now?'

'You are in no immediate danger. Our efforts are keeping your friend either under cover or on the move. He doesn't dare do anything now. If you stay put he won't dare come near you; if you keep running around you might walk right into him.'

'You say 'he'. Have you found something, Lieutenant?'

'Or she,' Dickerson shrugged. 'I say 'he' merely for convenience. Still, I can't conceive of a woman fooling around with mice, even dead ones. It's my hunch that the person who put the mouse on Miss Cassell's pillow and hid another under yours is of the male sex. I'll admit he might be working for a woman. A woman would be capable of thinking up a scheme of that sort, even if she might not be capable of executing it.'

Christopher inhaled slowly. 'I have an idea how it was done. The cat part, anyway.'

'Yes?' Dickerson's eyebrows lifted and his nostrils flared slightly. 'I'd like to hear it.'

'I think the sound of the cat was reproduced from a phonograph record. I think that he — that this person tortured a cat and had its cry recorded on one of those metal disc affairs. Then all he had to do was dial the number he wanted, wait until someone answered and if it was the right person, play the record.'

Dickerson nodded soberly. 'I'd thought of that as a possibility. It didn't seem logical to me that anyone could produce the desired effect at any given moment merely by twisting a cat's tail. I suppose the method suggests someone to you?'

Christopher's glance wavered a moment. 'Sorry. It does not.'

Dickerson's face became a touch more florid. 'Mr. Elliot, I believe I once told you I was sorry for you. I can't say that now. You are a man of sufficient intelligence to know of your jeopardy under the law. You should also have enough intelligence to know that the law can usually avenge but it cannot always protect. We can protect you if you co-operate with us, but we can't if you won't. It shouldn't be necessary for me to warn you that we may be dealing with a maniac.'

'We may be,' Christopher admitted.

'Then in heaven's name, man, give it up! Have some confidence in me. If you don't like me, go to the commissioner. Go to Kaufman, anyone you trust, but get off it. You have a wife and two children. When you stick your neck out, you are sticking theirs out too!'

Christopher did not answer, and they reached an end. When the cab finally pulled to the curb and Christopher saw that they were at police headquarters, he turned quickly and anger was on his lips. But Dickerson wasn't looking at him. Dickerson was chewing on his moustache and acting as if he might be more than a little fed up.

'We need your help,' Dickerson announced in a sighing voice. 'We won't keep you long.'

*   *   *

Connelly told him where to sit and what he was to do. 'When I give you the word,' Connelly warned, 'don't say anythin'. The intercom'll be on two ways an' we don't want to tip the show. We've had this guy on ice since noon an' he's been doin' a lot of thinkin'. An' we went to some trouble diggin' him up, so we don't want you to spoil it.'

Christopher nodded to show that he understood.

'Oh, you can talk now if you want.' Connelly waved. 'Just when I give you the word — say, what'd you do to the chief the other day, the day after we turned you loose? He came back here so mad he wouldn't even talk to McGhee!'

Christopher remembered and a flush mounted to his cheeks. 'I believe I misunderstood him. I thought he was trying to shake me down and I asked him how much he wanted.'

'You — ' Connelly stared.

'I wasn't quite myself.'

'Say — whew! I wouldn't want to've been you. The only reason the chief isn't a captain right now is — '

A red light blinked from the box on the desk. Connelly closed his mouth with a snap, lifted a warning hand, reached over and depressed a lever.

'Yeah, Chief?'

'Is McGhee there?'

'Yeah. Hey, McGhee, the chief wants you.'

Christopher did not see her, but over the interphone he heard a door open and close, and he heard footsteps cross bare floor. He was puzzled until he realized that they were two offices removed from Dickerson and that whoever was in there was being made to think this end of the phone was on the other side of the partition.

A chair scraped and a pad rustled. 'Sorry to keep you waiting,' Dickerson's voice said. 'This is Miss McGhee. Don't be afraid to speak out so she can hear you.'

'I'll speak out all right!' The voice was angry. 'I'd like to know what's the idea, holding me here all afternoon!'

'Sorry, Malloy, but it couldn't be helped. I won't detain you any longer than necessary. Just a few routine questions and then you can go.'

'Questions?' He didn't sound so angry now. 'Oh, no, Lieutenant. What do you take me for, a chump? I'm a business

261

man. Any questions you have to ask me — '

Christopher's mouth went dry. He would have risen had not Connelly's hand held him down.

' — you can ask my lawyer. If you want it any plainer than that, Lieutenant, you can go to hell. Yes, Miss, you heard what I said. Or would you like me to speak a little louder?'

There was a bumping scrape as of a chair pushed back. 'All right, Malloy.' Dickerson's voice. 'If that's the way you feel about it, I'll turn you over to MacFarlane.'

'Do that, Lieutenant. It would be a pleasure. Just cook me for a couple of hours under the sun lamp and we'll see how it looks tomorrow when I go see a certain friend of mine. We don't need to mention any names, do we, Lieutenant?'

This time Christopher got up, but Connelly had already released the lever.

When they reached Dickerson's office they found that large gentleman in the act of closing the corridor door. He turned slowly and his grey eyes held question.

'It was Axelrod,' Christopher declared flatly.

Dickerson nodded, crossed over and sat at his desk. 'I thought so. I wanted you to identify his voice so we could be certain.'

Christopher sat down. He felt slightly weak. 'How did you do it? How in the world did you catch him? Where did you pick him up?'

Dickerson wet his moustache with his lower lip. 'When you first told me about it, I thought it sounded like Bud Malloy's work. Malloy is a private investigator. We've almost had him before on a couple of attempted shakedowns, but he's been a little too slick for us. Where the victims squawk we can usually nail his racket although I have no doubt there are some who haven't squawked and have probably had to pay.' Dickerson frowned. 'Did you pay him any money?'

'No.'

'Then we can't do much with him on that angle. However, we're definitely certain he's the one who was tailing Ruth Cassell. We've established him near her apartment house and, more important, in the vicinity of the boarding house where she was last hiding. Apparently he picked up her trail Monday when she went shopping on Grant Avenue. And finally, we've traced him to Lumson's Chop House on Ward Avenue on the night and at about the time she was killed. The cab driver who brought her there saw Malloy leave another cab and enter the restaurant after her.'

'But he walked out of here!' Christopher was halfway to his feet. 'You let him get away!'

'Nobody gets away, Mr. Elliot. Malloy's in that room right now, sitting in the three-legged chair and trying to dodge the locomotive headlight; you'll be apt to remember them. And if he happens to have anything on his mind, it will be just too bad.'

'You mean you think Malloy killed her?'

'I mean that whoever Malloy has been working for, this person you've been protecting, will be known. Malloy will sing. He can't do anything else. He knows there's a hot seat waiting at the end of this one and he won't cover for anyone. Not even if it might happen to be your wife, or you.'

'Me? I don't understand, Lieutenant.'

'You could have hired him. He might have gotten out of hand.'

'Oh, no. I didn't hire him. I had nothing to do with him. I've never even seen him. I've heard his voice only twice. The second time was here, just now, over your interphone.'

'All right. Your wife, then.'

'Wrong. My wife did not hire him or anyone.'

'How can you be sure?'

'Because he wasn't in it until I had broken off with Ruth; he didn't enter it at all until Ruth took the cottage in Chelmere less than a month ago. At that time I wasn't seeing Ruth. If Henrietta had ever intended to hire a detective she would have done so six months before, when I was giving her cause.'

'Don't you suppose your wife might have resented the other woman's moving into her neighbourhood? Don't you think that when Ruth Cassell came to Chelmere it was about time for your wife to do something if she was going to do anything at all? Maybe she hoped, during those first six months, that you would get over your infatuation. But when the girl came to Echo Road and started calling you on the telephone, it was a different matter.'

Christopher was silent.

Dickerson got up from his chair and came around the desk. His face and eyes were sober as he looked down. 'We have hundreds of men who are trained for this sort of work. We have the finest laboratory equipment money can buy. We use the latest methods known to science. We have experts of every description: forensic chemists, ballistics men, pathologists, psychiatrists, toxicologists, graphologists and others covering every branch of investigation.

'In spite of what you may have read or might believe, we are efficient. In this city last year ninety-three homicides were committed and of that number only four are still in the unsolved file. We have made mistakes, but the margin of error is constantly narrowing. Our job is criminal investigation; yours is designing houses. What do you think you can find by yourself? If you found anything, would you know what it was? Would you even know if you found it?'

Dickerson bent down and put his hands on Christopher's shoulders. 'For the last time, Elliot,' he said pleadingly, 'give it up.'

★   ★   ★

A thin finger of moon spent itself in lending a dull glaze to the windows of the dark house and had little left for lawn or road. The house was a shapeless blot against the dark sky and behind and below it the tops of trees were a turbulent stream rushing down to a sea of blackness.

In the valley below, the white cottage was a faint, chimerical blur.

Christopher let out his breath and would have left the deep shadow of the terrace had he not heard a sound. Faintly at first, a warning borne on the rustling breeze, and growing steadily in volume. A car was approaching, beginning the steep ascent.

He pulled back, hugging and compressing himself against the house.

The beams of headlights appeared, sweeping an arc about the curve and throwing into bold momentary relief the trunks of trees, an open field, the garage at the roadside. For a fleeting moment the terrace was filled with a dim reflected radiance, and then he was safe again.

The car crunched to a stop. A door banged. A shoe broke a pebble with a pinging snap and a silhouetted figure loomed on the walk.

'Lyman!' Cissie Folwell's barroom voice shattered the quiet.

The figure turned. 'Yes, dear?'

'You'd better bring a needle, too. I forgot to buy one today. The old one's worn out!'

'Yes, dear.'

Ashton passed him by, so near Christopher could hear the other's breathing. He heard the sound of the key in the lock and of the door scraping inward. He glanced about and realized that he was standing in front of double French doors. He moved, just in time, for light blazed within and made a bright square where he had been.

He moved again, risking detection, bringing his head around until he could see through the narrow aperture between marquisette curtain and door stile. He saw Ashton cross to the phonograph, open the cabinet it rested on and select a few albums. Then Ashton lifted the lid of the machine and unscrewed the needle from the playing arm. Putting the needle in his waistcoat pocket he gathered albums and crossed the room.

Christopher was standing erect, in the safer ell between wall and fireplace chimney, when Ashton closed and locked the front door and started up the path.

'Did you bring some good ones?' Cissie called.

Ashton held his reply until he was nearer the car. 'I brought the Rimsky-Korsakovs and the Tchaikovskys. I'm sure you'll like them.'

269

'Yes, well, you know me. I'd rather hear the hot stuff. Benny Goodman or Woody Herman. But I suppose we've got to do something to please Henrietta.'

In his corner of darkness, Christopher shivered.

The car backed and turned and headlights swept the terrace. He was protected by the chimney and he remained without breathing until Ashton had completed the turn and the head-lights were going away. When the car negotiated the curve on the downgrade he stepped out and walked to the low stone wall on the roadside. He watched the headlights diminish in the distance, and when the red rear light had vanished he loosened a stone from the wall, lifted it and carried it with him to the double French doors.

⋆   ⋆   ⋆

He turned the lens of his flashlight floorward and guardedly switched it on. In the resultant glow he could discern objects and he moved carefully so as to avoid them. The position of the phonograph he knew, but there were other equally important things he wanted to find. From previous visits he remembered that Ashton had a desk and it was not in this room. It was on the other side in the room intended for a breakfast nook that Ashton had rigged up as his studio.

He crossed over cautiously and was at the entrance to the front hallway when, right beside him, the telephone began to ring.

He froze.

He'd made that mistake once before, answering a telephone. He couldn't afford any mistakes now. He relaxed, and ignoring the summons, continued on. He passed through the dining room, pushed back a swing door and stood in Ashton's improvised studio.

Quickly he moved to the window, pulled down the shade and then, retracing, closed the door and turned on the overhead lights.

The telephone stopped ringing.

He returned the flashlight to his pocket. Going to the desk, he began pulling out drawers, riffling through papers, searching for just what he wasn't sure.

In the second drawer of the desk's pedestal he found an album, crammed with photographs. His heart leaped. He opened it and turned a few pages and then his elation turned to dismay. There were so many pictures that, if he scanned each one, the task of searching all would require an hour or more. He skipped pages. The first part held photographs taken by Ashton on his travels. The Mediterranean, France, Italy, Africa, Egypt the Levant — no good.

He turned to the middle, working faster, scanning more hurriedly. The pictures here seemed mixed-up and meaningless, without plan. Ashton on a horse. A bearded man, holding a rifle. Ashton in mackinaw shirt and moccasins, frying eggs in an iron griddle over a campfire. Ashton holding up a lake trout.

Two photographs of a different colour: newer and brighter than the rest. One, a snapshot of this house; the other, Ashton's roadster.

Christopher eyed them in bewilderment. As mixed-up as the photographs in this section were, certainly those didn't belong. They were newer, of an entirely different period. And then he stopped breathing.

Lake trout and a camp-fire; mackinaw shirt and moccasins; a man with a rifle —

Brentwood Lakes!

He held the album by its covers and shook it vigorously. Nothing fell out. He thrust the album aside and rummaged wildly, pulling items from the drawers and leaving them scattered in wild disorder.

Nothing.

There were shelves containing hundreds of books and he glared at them, trying to pierce their jackets, to see through their covers and pages and fathom if the missing snapshots might be hidden there. He spotted two of Ashton's: *Lonely Highway* and *Dark is the Night*. He pulled them out roughly, shook them and found nothing.

He would have turned elsewhere in frustrated wrath had he not noticed a slight division in the pages in the top of one of the books. Eagerly he snatched it out only to return it in disappointment.

The division was caused by a newspaper clipping.

But that gave him a method, and he moved systematically along the shelves, examining the tops of the books. He came to a copy of *Troilus and Cressida*, found the telltale slight separation and pulled it out. And then he was trembling, for in his hand was the yellowed snapshot of a girl. The girl was wearing a bathing suit and was sitting on the end of a diving board. She was laughing and apparently protesting against having her picture taken.

The girl was Ruth Cassell.

Straightening, he carefully replaced the snapshot in the book and returned the book to its shelf. Leaving the disarray of the desk as it was he turned out the light and crossed swiftly to the living room.

He stopped by the phonograph. The machine was a portable electric model, covered with pigskin, equipped with a device for playing a dozen records without manual change. He dropped to his knees and began a thorough search of the cabinet beneath. When he had finished he went through again, faster at first and finally with frenzied speed. He extended his search to other parts of the room and then to other parts of the house. Wherever he found drawer or door he opened and rummaged.

He was back in the living room, glaring in baffled rage, when he heard the slam of a car door. Swiftly he moved and passed through the shattered French door to the terrace. Risking discovery he crossed over the terrace and dropped behind the low stone wall.

When he heard the key in the lock and the inward scrape of the door he rose up from the wall and began running along the road. Reaching the turn, he kept straight on through the woods.

He was safely away, but he had not found the principle object of his search: the round metal disc he had been so sure he would find.

9

It was morning. The hands of the clock had not yet reached the hour of eight, but they were crowded in Dickerson's office as thick as relatives at the reading of a will. MacFarlane, he of the fat smooth cheeks, the cat-like walk and the maddening voice, was reading the transcript that McGhee was waiting for. Connelly was holding on to a uniformed patrolman with one hand, to a cup of coffee with the other, and the while he was casting worried, questioning glances in the chief's direction.

The door opened, banging into Connelly's back and spilling some of the coffee. Schultz, of Recovery, stuck his head in, scowled around and withdrew.

MacFarlane pointed to a paragraph in the transcript. 'This is what he objects to,' MacFarlane told McGhee. 'He insists he didn't try to shake Elliot down. He claims he made Elliot a straight business proposition, and that it was Elliot who called him first. He knows that we know he's lying, but what can you do with a guy like that? He'd get in front of a jury and moan about police persecution and if there were any women on the jury they'd believe him.' He turned his head. 'How about it, Joe? Is it okay to let Malloy duck the attempted shakedown?'

Dickerson glanced up from the newspapers. 'Hm? Oh, Malloy. What's the matter, won't he sign it?'

'Not with the shakedown in it, he won't, and that's the only part of it that amounts to anything.'

'What about his principal? Will he say who he was working for?'

'He won't sing, Joe. He knows we haven't got enough on him. He is absolutely alibied. He never went through the Chop House. He claims he thought the girl might've gone to the ladies' room and he waited for her to come out. He's got three witnesses including Lumson himself.'

'Hm.' Dickerson worried his moustache. 'In other words, Malloy has a pretty good idea of who killed the girl and intends to cash in on it if we should slip up.'

'That's about the way it reads, Joe.'

'All right. Leave the transcript as it is.'

MacFarlane started to say something else, changed his mind and, shrugging, handed the typescript to McGhee. 'Let her go as is,' he said.

When McGhee left, Connelly could see the chief a bit more clearly. Dickerson was reading the newspaper, apparently unmindful of the fact that at least seventeen thousand things had to be done and that within five minutes the first of them would require his presence at the railway station. Connelly drained the last of the coffee and tried to get up enough courage to interrupt him.

MacFarlane said, 'Joe, I think I'll — '

Dickerson's fist hit the desk with a bang. He jumped from his chair and his usually florid face was grey. His hand described a sweeping arc, hit the interphone with a thump, fumbled, found the lever and depressed it.

'McGhee!'

Click. 'Yes, Lieutenant?'

'McGhee, listen. Get me the telephone detail — no. Go straight to the wire chief. I want the location and name for Grant two-seven-four-three-four. Have you got that? Grant two-seven-four-three-four. And hurry!'

'Yes, Lieutenant.'

MacFarlane inched nearer the desk. 'What the hell's wrong now, Joe?'

Dickerson held up the newspaper and pointed a shaking finger. From grey he had gone to purple. 'That damned fool Elliot. He's really done it now. Look at this!'

After MacFarlane gave up trying to reach across the desk and decided to walk around it he managed to get the newspaper. Connelly and the patrolman crowded in, and then MacFarlane, puzzled, asked, 'Where? What is it? I don't see anything.'

'That display ad, at the top of the column — here, let me have it!' Dickerson grabbed the paper. 'Listen to this: *Will the little boy or girl living in suburban Chelmere who has had several white mice stolen within the past few weeks please get in touch with me by calling Grant two-seven-four-three-four and claim a reward of five dollars?'* Dickerson crumpled the newspaper and slammed it to the floor.

'Kind of working that mouse gag overtime, isn't he?' MacFarlane asked.

'It's no gag, Mac.' Dickerson's grey eyes were dark and bitingly direct. 'Believe me, there's one live cat and two dead mice at the bottom of this mess, and behind them is a maniac. I only wished to heaven it was a gag.' He kicked at the crumpled newspaper and gave his moustache a vicious tug.

MacFarlane's pink cheeks went pale. 'In that case, Joe, we've got to do something. Fast.'

'Right. Some boy or girl is in terrible danger. We don't know who it is; only the maniac knows who it is.'

They looked at each other, and in each other's eyes read thoughts. They had knowledge, skill, radio, laboratories, machines, hundreds of trained men, but they were helpless.

'Mac,' Dickerson said, 'I'm going to turn this part of it over to you. As soon as McGhee comes through with the location of that phone, grab one of the telephone men and a monitor set-up and go there. Notify the Chelmere and State Police to stand by, and if a call from the kid comes through find out where he lives and see that he gets protection. Plain clothes if possible. We don't want to scare the bird off, but at any cost protect the kid.'

MacFarlane nodded. 'Okay, Joe.'

'Connelly and I will be at the station if anything turns up.' His strong lower teeth caught at his moustache. 'I only hope we're not too late.'

★ ★ ★

'All right,' Dickerson announced. 'That row is all clear. What have we left?'

Connelly looked up from his pad. 'This one here, unless it should happen to be one of the upper rows. Then we'll have to start all over again.'

Dickerson ignored the inference. He signalled to the patient man with the master key and stepped back to give him room. Around them, held back by a handful of uniformed patrolmen and railway police, was the mob. The mob and the press; wherever it might be, they were always at hand. Start in the middle of a field or in the bottom of a quarry, and in five minutes the mob and the press would be there.

They had been good-humoured. They were expressing themselves in wise cracks. 'What are you looking for, Joe?' The press knew him, and the public took it up.

What do you expect to find, Joe?

As if he himself knew.

'Okay, Joe. Number thirty. Suitcase, raincoat, umbrella, pair of galoshes — ' The stuff came out and was spread on the stone floor. Dickerson bent down, looked to the rear of the locker, returned to a kneeling position, probed with hands and eyes, shook his head.

Give you two bucks for the raincoat, Joe!

Dickerson grinned.

'Okay. Number twenty-seven. Two

282

cartons of groceries — '.

Down again. Search, probe, seek — for what? He stood and dusted his knees. 'No. Not there.'

Have they got any butter, Joe?

Dickerson grinned again, but the grin was beginning to hurt.

The mob bulged and parted to let a man through. He came straight over, sought out Dickerson and said swiftly, 'The number is registered to a Miss Margaret O'Bannigan. She's Elliot's secretary. He's borrowed her place for the day. It's an apartment in the Garden Plaza. MacFarlane is set up there now with Blake of Telephone.'

'O'Bannigan, Garden Plaza.' Dickerson nodded thoughtfully. 'Thanks.'

The man was swallowed up by the mob, and the patient fellow with the master key said, 'Okay. Number twenty-four. Suitcase and rubbers — ' He paused. He glanced up at Dickerson with puzzled eyes and suddenly moved out of the way.

Dickerson was on his knees, then lunging forward. He came up bearing a crumpled paper sack. The sack was heavy. In it was the outline of something that was hard, and of something else that was soft. With trembling hands he opened the sack, drew out a glove just far enough to see the bloodstain inside the palm of it and hastily put it back.

★   ★   ★

They were back in Dickerson's office, and if possible even more people were around the desk than had been before. McGhee was busy with string tags; a short, bald man was holding a paper bag, a fresh one; a long and cadaverously thin man was putting on rubber gloves; a slender youth held wet photographic prints, and Connelly was hanging on to his fourth cup of coffee for the morning.

'All right, Pfeifer,' Dickerson announced. 'You get the bag and the gloves. You'll give Schultz the dope so he can start tracking down the bag. I don't know how far Rosenbaum can get with the gloves; they look pretty old to me, but let him try anyway.'

The short bald man dexterously caught

the exhibits in his fresh paper bag. 'I'll have a preliminary report in an hour,' he promised and marched out.

'You, DeMarco, get the rod.'

The thin man smiled. Grasping the butt of the pistol between gloved thumb and forefinger he raised it and said, 'Harrington and Richardson twenty-two calibre. New Defender.' He wrinkled his nose. 'It has been fired since last cleaned. Unfortunately this type of pistol has no front sight, so that the thread and fibre test will be useless. However, we'll give it a whirl.'

DeMarco made his exit, the slender youth left the photographic prints, McGhee went her weary way, and only Connelly and Dickerson remained.

Connelly drank some coffee and wiped his mouth with the back of his hand. 'Chief,' he asked, 'what do you think?'

Dickerson stood up. 'I'll tell you after we've been to the Garden Plaza,' he answered. 'I don't like the looks of things. I don't like them at all.'

★   ★   ★

It was quite some time before Christopher Elliot realized just who the fat, pink-cheeked man was. He had introduced himself as MacFarlane and had then gone to sit at the other telephone, dividing the headset with Blake. MacFarlane didn't say much, and that was why it took him so long to make the discovery. When he realized that this fat, pink man seated across from him was the Voice, the one who had been directing the show from behind the floodlight, he became cold with anger. He stared steadily until MacFarlane could no longer ignore him. MacFarlane grinned at first; then, annoyed, he shrugged and turned his back.

The telephone kept them busy. It seemed to be ringing all the time. At first Christopher had been elated, scarcely able to control himself in answering. But when he began to get the gist of the calls he cooled down. After a short while his answers to inquiries became routine.

Cranks. Stupid people. Lonely people. People with nothing to do. Nothing in prospect but to call and answer an advertisement that piqued their curiosity. Some of them went into great detail in describing the mice they had lost. He would have been more convinced if they hadn't wanted to keep on talking long past all logical bounds.

There was one woman who wanted to marry him because she knew he would be kind to every living creature.

The first really youthful voice he heard — it was a girl — almost drove him out of his skin. He signalled frantically, and MacFarlane and the telephone man heard it too and were straining at their ear phones. And then it developed the girl had had two mice and her older brother had let the cat get them. They hadn't exactly been stolen, but she'd lost them. She didn't want the five dollars, but she wouldn't mind having some more mice, or maybe rabbits this time.

Christopher sighed and settled down to wait.

At half-past nine the telephone rang again; it was at least the twentieth call in an hour and he lifted the receiver wearily.

'Yes?'

There was no answer. The line was alive, he knew, for he could detect the faint sound of breathing. He glanced sharply across at MacFarlane. MacFarlane was listening, too, a puzzled expression on his fat pink face.

'Who are you? What do you want?'

A gentle sigh, a click, and then the dial tone.

Christopher nearly jumped from his chair. 'That was he! It was our man! I'll swear it was. He pulled exactly the same stunt on me when I was at the cottage on Echo Road!'

'Take it easy, Mr. Elliot,' MacFarlane advised. 'It might be your man, and again it might not. You've had twenty cranks in an hour. Any of them might be the man, too; anything is possible in a case like this. We can't afford to gamble. When you get a *bona fide* answer to your ad we'll have something to go on. Slow down or you'll have a stroke.'

Christopher glared at him, remembered that he was the Voice, and remembered also that his anger was silent.

From then on no further word passed between them. When the telephone rang, Christopher answered it and steadily his hopes diminished and his anger grew.

At five minutes before ten, Dickerson came in.

★ ★ ★

Dickerson's first questioning glance was toward MacFarlane and when he received a negative answer he turned to Christopher.

'Mr. Elliot,' Dickerson was grave and ominously quiet, 'I warned you to stay off this thing. If I had realized yesterday that you would go so far as to advertise in the newspaper, I would have remanded you to jail, regardless of later consequences. Do you know what you've done?'

'What I've done? No, what have I done?'

'I warned you that we might be working with a maniac. He knows where he got the mice. If he sees that ad he'll likely figure that we're going to find out where he got them. Perhaps the circumstances are such that as soon as we learn the source of the mice we will also learn who he is. To prevent disclosure he may kill. The fact that it's a child won't stop him. Don't you realize how you may be jeopardizing the life of a child?'

'I — I hadn't thought of it in that way.'

'For your sake, Mr. Elliot, I hope to God your hunch about this thing is wrong. But I don't know.' Dickerson slowly shook his head. Abruptly facing about he went over to sit with MacFarlane.

★ ★ ★

At eleven o'clock the telephone sounded its thirty-fifth summons of the morning. There was nothing in this to distinguish it from the others. A short, sharp ring, and when he lifted the receiver the burring rattle continued in the earpiece. Over at the table Dickerson had replaced MacFarlane; the lieutenant and the telephone man were already listening in bored disinterest, sharing the headset.

When the rattle subsided Christopher said, 'Hello?'

'We have a collect call from Chelmere. Will you accept it?'

Chelmere! The first of the day. At the table the three men lost their disinterest and poised in a huddled, watchful group.

'Yes, I'll accept the call.'

A buzz and a click. A boy's voice, thin with suppressed excitement: 'My name is Bobby Thompson and my father saw an ad in the paper this morning, and my mice were stolen, all five of them, last week Monday — '

'Find out where he lives!' Dickerson's voice held agonized pleading.

' — and I want the five dollars' reward, please.'

'You'll get it, Bobby my boy.' So they think I'm crazy? So they want to humour me? 'Where were your mice stolen from, Bobby?'

'From the back porch, where mama made me keep them.'

'And where do you live?'

'On Crescent Street in Chelmere, two blocks down from the Folwell Museum.

It's the corner house.'

'All right, Bobby. You'll get your five dollars today.'

He hung up, and suddenly he was exhausted. At the other table, orders were issuing from Dickerson in a steady stream. The lieutenant looked a little like a man in a play; he was bouncing like a madman, trying to call three numbers at once, and somehow doing it.

Christopher pulled himself from his momentary stupor. There was one more job he must do, one more detail before he could stop. A telephone directory lay on his desk and rapidly he fanned it, searching until he found the number he must call.

The end now was rushing in with incredible speed —

'Doctor Swinburne? This is Christopher Elliot.'

'Oh, yes, Mr. Elliot! I called your office about an hour ago and they gave me a number to call, but each time I tried to reach you the line was busy. I have the information you wanted. Do you have pencil and paper handy?'

Christopher found a pencil in his pocket, wet the point of it and attempted to steady his hand. 'Go ahead,' he instructed.

'The mouse was brought in by the Reverend Millis, Five-Twenty-Eight Ridge Road, Chelmere. It was the second one found in the house of one of his parishioners, a Mrs. Clarence Holmes, at Five-Forty-Six Ridge Road, Chelmere. After this second mouse had been found on her pillow, the woman refused to remain in the house. The reverend suspected a lunatic of trying to drive her insane. The mouse had died of carbon-monoxide gas poisoning, same cause as the one in your case. Does that help you?'

'It does. I can't thank you enough.'

'Not at all. Glad I could find it.'

Mrs. Clarence Holmes, a lonely, frightened woman. It was beginning to fit now. Five-Forty-Six Ridge Road was the house Lyman Ashton had bought, the one that had suddenly become available after he had been dickering for the white cottage on Echo Road —

He broke off sharply to discover that Dickerson was staring at him. Dickerson's ordinarily florid face was quite pale and his eyes were almost completely black.

'Did you hear what Swinburne said?' Christopher could not resist a note of triumph.

Dickerson's eyes wavered. He shook himself and inhaled a sighing breath, 'I heard it. Come along. We're ready to leave for Chelmere.'

★ ★ ★

The two cars that they filled travelled without sirens or escort, but they travelled fast. Both were equipped with two-way radio, and Dickerson, who sat in the rear seat of the second car between Christopher Elliot and Connelly, outlined his plan.

'MacFarlane, your car will go in first,' Dickerson spoke into the microphone. 'Leave it at the foot of Crescent Street and have your men walk up toward the Thompson house one at a time, at intervals of two minutes. Assign them by compass points so they can best cover all sides of the house and the streets. It won't be easy in daylight, but keep them out of sight as much as possible. If it should become necessary to enter the house, you'll be the man and the rest cover the outside. Got it?'

'Got it,' MacFarlane's voice came from the speaker. 'What about the local that's in the house now?'

'We'll pull him out. Considering this morning's blank phone call and assuming that our party might have made it, it's safer than an even bet he's keeping tabs on the place, watching his chance. He probably knows, or has guessed that we've contacted the Thompson boy by now. So we'll try a trick. This car will drive right up to the house, giving him plenty of opportunity to count us if he's watching that close. We'll go in, stay a few minutes and come back out bringing the Chelmere man with us. Then we'll drive off. That leaves your outfit in charge. If your men are sufficiently hidden we may fool him.'

'Sounds okay. How long do we maintain the plant?'

'Until tomorrow morning if necessary. The men in this car will relieve your group one at a time. We'll operate out of Chelmere police headquarters, and as soon as you have your set-up complete, check with me there.'

'This guy Thompson,' MacFarlane's voice said, 'will probably be home for lunch. You'd better tell him to head straight for the front door when he comes home from work tonight. We don't want to make any mistakes.'

The radio connection was broken then, and the distance between the speeding cars began perceptibly to widen. Neither Dickerson nor Connelly seemed to have anything further to say and the two men in the front seat continued to be completely unconcerned.

Christopher, riding into he knew not what, could not help but shudder as the full significance of MacFarlane's final remark came home to him.

* * *

296

It was twenty minutes past noon by the dash clock when they ground to a stop in front of the Thompson home. Christopher followed Dickerson and Connelly from the rear seat and, acting under previous instructions, went a little way off by himself. The two in front stepped out and flexed their legs. One of them walked around, obviously inspecting tyres; the other lingered by the hood, lifted it and became absorbed in a study of the engine.

Christopher knew that four men were stationed in the immediate vicinity, keeping watch on the house. Despite the fact that he knew this, it was broad daylight, and there seemed to be scarcely enough cover anywhere to hide a cat, the only person in sight was a man spooning leaves from the storm sewer at the intersection of Crescent and Peach, on the Donaths' corner two blocks away.

Dickerson and Connelly had started up the path and Christopher hurried to join them. They reached the porch and stood diffidently, and by prearrangement Christopher pulled at the doorbell.

The door was opened almost at once

by Officer Skaggs of the Chelmere police. He saw and recognized Christopher and gave him a doubtful 'Hello.' Then he saw Dickerson and pulled the door open wide.

They filed into the hall and came to a living room separated from the dining room by a wide portal. The Thompsons were seated about a table, having lunch, but it was plain they weren't enjoying it. Thompson, a red-faced auto dealer whom Christopher knew by sight, appeared anxious and ill at ease, and his angular, jaundiced wife acted downright scared.

The Thompson boy, who was perhaps three years older than Wickie, slid from his chair and ran around the table to meet them.

'Robert!'

'But they said I'd get five dollars!' the boy protested. He stood his ground. But he was confused, for he did not know to whom he should look for payment.

Christopher did not need Dickerson's prompting glance. Already he was reaching in his pocket. He found his wallet, pulled out five crisp one-dollar bills and held them out to the boy.

'Here you are, Bobby. I'm the man who promised it to you. I'm very grateful to you for calling. I'm also thankful to you, Mr. Thompson, for reading the advertisement and telling your son about it.'

'Look!' The boy held the money aloft and ran with it back to the table. 'Five bucks! Gee!'

'Five *dollars*, Robert.' Mrs. Thompson's sallow cheeks flushed painfully.

Thompson seemed somewhat mollified. 'I thought at first it might be a gag,' he admitted. 'But I didn't realize it was going to cause all this ruckus. What's it all about? What have Bobby's mice got to do with it?'

Dickerson loomed, an imposing figure, framed by the wide doorway. 'Don't be alarmed. It doesn't amount to very much.' His manner and voice were soothing. 'I feel that I owe you an apology. We're sorry for intruding in this way. We have only a few questions to ask, and then we'll leave you alone.'

Thompson put his napkin down. 'You

mean you're going to pull Skaggs out of here? There's a murder mixed up in this, ain't there?'

'There's really no cause for alarm.' Dickerson's reproving glance at Officer Skaggs was quickly covered. 'You can go on about your work in the usual way. The person who stole the mice was probably just some harmless nut.'

'Harmless?' Thompson sputtered. 'You call it harmless, him killing that girl?'

'Now, Mr. Thompson. You know how the newspapers are. Give them an attractive girl and a few mysterious circumstances — you couldn't expect them to miss a chance like that for a good story. Now, lad, tell me. You said your mice were kept on the back porch. What did you keep them in?'

'In a round box that cheese had come in,' the boy answered promptly. 'It was a wooden box. I cut a square hole in the top and put copper screen wire over it.'

Dickerson produced pad and pencil and sketched rapidly. 'You mean one of those round four-pound containers, the kind that usually holds Edam cheese?'

Bobby turned appealing eyes on his father.

'That's the kind,' Thompson admitted, crossly. 'If it ain't important, what difference does it make?'

'A theft is a theft, regardless of whether it's mice or jewellery or an automobile. Now, Bobby, do you recall if anyone took particular interest in your mice? That is, anyone outside of your family or friends?'

'Sure. All the kids did.'

'I'm more interested in grown-ups. Someone, perhaps, who happened to come by while you were feeding them or playing with them out on the back porch.'

The boy screwed up his face in thought. 'Well, I don't know as there was. Mr. Renault, the postman, and Mr. Geer, from up to the museum, they watched me feed 'em a couple of times. There might've been somebody else, but I can't remember.'

If Dickerson felt Christopher's tension he chose to ignore it. He had finished the sketch and he held the pad out. 'Does this look anything like the cage?'

Bobby came around, took the pad and

brought it to his father. Together they examined Dickerson's work, and together they nodded.

Smiling his blandest smile, Dickerson retrieved the pad. 'Thank you very much for your co-operation. As I said before, there's nothing to worry about. Just some harmless crank. We'll have him before long. Good day, and thank you very much.' Then he turned and with a movement of head and eyes perceptible only to those in the living room, denoted that they were to follow him out.

When Thompson saw that Skaggs was leaving, he hastily pushed away from the table. 'Hey! Wait a minute — '

They had reached the porch and were trooping down the steps when Thompson gained the door.

'You mean,' he was almost shouting, 'you're not going to leave *anybody* here?'

Dickerson turned and smiled blandly. 'Nothing to worry about, I assure you. Good day, Mr. Thompson!'

They crammed into the car, and when they were underway Dickerson removed his hat and wiped his forehead with his coat-sleeve.

'You couldn't ask for anything better than that,' Dickerson sighed. 'If our man is anywhere near the place, he ought to be convinced.'

Connelly's long face became involved in a look of admiration. 'Say, that Thompson guy is sure a good actor.'

'He is,' Dickerson agreed, 'except that he wasn't acting. I didn't dare let them know we're watching the place. It would be all over town in an hour.'

★　★　★

When they reached Chelmere police station, Dickerson glanced in some vexation at Christopher. It was evident that he didn't know just what to do with him.

'If it's all right with you,' Christopher suggested, 'I'll run up to my house and get some more linen. I'm down to my last shirt again.'

'Sounds like a good idea. Whatever you do, stay away from the Thompson place.

You can join us here later, if you'd like. We'll probably eat sometime. By the bye, what were the numbers of those houses on Ridge Road, the ones Swinburne mentioned?'

'The Reverend Millis, at Five-Twenty-Eight, and Lyman Ashton, at Five-Forty-Six.'

Skaggs had gotten out of the car and was hovering on the curb, waiting for Dickerson. Suddenly he flushed, stepped from the curb and stuck his head through the open car window.

'Meant to tell you this before,' Skaggs announced, 'but things have been happenin' a little too fast — This mornin' that fellow Ashton you just mentioned. He was in here, wantin' police protection. It's another one of them damned mice. Somebody broke into his house last night and put a mouse on his pillow.'

★   ★   ★

He stopped at his house, but it wasn't shirts he was seeking. The house was cold and damply empty; he knew, even without consulting the thermostat, that the burner was exhausted of oil. He removed topcoat, jacket and waistcoat and shivered violently while he searched. He opened bureau drawers and closets and his efforts were futile until at last he thought of the chest beneath the window in the upper hall.

He found a sweater, a crew-neck pullover, and drew it on; he found also a cap and a pair of tight-fitting pigskin gloves, and then he left the house.

When he reached Crescent Street he began the slow ascent and as he passed the Folwell Museum he wondered if Wick might be working there. He wondered, too, if Wick might suspect that the police would soon be with him and that he who had sneered so mightily would now have to answer and explain his interest in a little boy's mice. That should be good. Wick would attempt, first, to patronize Dickerson, and then he would try to freeze him, and in the end even MacFarlane might get him.

No, not the Voice. That was too good.

He came by the ridiculous little park in

which Frank Folwell's marble statue stared in eternal contempt at the rooftops of the village which had spawned him. Frank Folwell, concocter of a noxious brew and builder of an evil wall; a man whose only memorials had been constructed at his own behest and then only because his widow could find no loophole of escape from the strict provisions of his will.

He passed beyond the park into a wooded stretch and when the iron gates were in sight he left the road and entered the woods.

The ladder remained upright this time, but he dared not risk using it. The ground was further down on the inside of the wall and sloped sharply away, and he feared the ladder might get him in serious trouble. He squirmed from the top, let himself down to arm's length, hung suspended a moment, kicked and let go. He landed in the soft loamy soil, rolled and then was swiftly up, running for the cover of trees.

This time, if there were any new aches or pains he did not feel them. He was beyond feeling anything but a wild, pounding elation. He had beaten the wall twice; this time he would beat the house too. And if the muscular thug who stood guard should reappear, this time there would be no surprise to handicap him, for he was ready.

He reached the cover of the garage, crept along the wall of it, and then he saw the thug. The chunky man was in the parking area between garage and house; he was wearing hip-length rubber boots and his muscular arms were driving his huge hands to polish Lyman Ashton's roadster. His broad back was toward Christopher and for a moment he straightened, resting, and glanced up to watch the smoke curling from the central chimney of the house.

Christopher grinned, reached down, found a small stone and threw it with unerring accuracy.

He was flat against the wall when the thug came lumbering by; his extended foot fouled the rubber boots and the man went sprawling headlong.

Christopher stepped from the garage

side and stood balanced, waiting. The other grunted, sat up and looked dazedly around. Christopher stepped nearer in a feinting movement and the other did not move; the small, stupid eyes seemed fogged and the bullet head shook impatiently as if to clear them. Christopher feinted nearer and the other lunged suddenly; his move was fingertips short and Christopher laughed and danced away.

Bellowing in rage the chunky man scrambled to his feet and came rushing in, trying to pin him to the garage wall. Christopher got his back to the wall and slid along it, and this time he turned and his left fist sank to the wrist in the other's belly.

The fat ape let out a squawk and tried another rush and his jaw collided hard with Christopher's right fist. The blow sent a knife of pain through Christopher's arm to his shoulder, but it didn't seem to bother the thug. Christopher sidestepped, turned and moved in to meet a new rush, sinking another left in the inviting paunch.

This time the ape's face grimaced in pain.

Whatever doubt might have been in Christopher's mind was gone now. He carried the fight forward, flailing that bouncing midriff with both hands. The other began to sag. He tried to cover his stomach and Christopher butted him full in the face with the top of his head.

The other's hands came up with an agonized jerk.

Christopher aimed carefully, leaned, and planted a hundred and eighty pounds of solid right on the squat man's fleshy throat.

He went down as if felled with a crowbar.

Christopher drew back, panting, and leaned against the garage for support. He was very tired, and the paralysis of fatigue was swiftly claiming him. His hands were so heavy he could hardly lift them. Suddenly he began to heave and tremble, and had the other man been able to get up he could not have defended himself.

But the stocky man did not get up. He lay twitching on his back, struggled, managed to roll over to his stomach and presently began to crawl, blindly, toward the sloping hollow that led to the wall.

A maid, a butler and cook were in the kitchen and his sudden appearance frightened them to immobility. He had regained control of his breathing enough to speak, and he said, 'You know who I am. Where is my wife?'

The butler's face was nearly as white as the sink he was holding on to for support. His free hand made a pawing, defensive gesture. 'Mrs. Elliot's in the l-library, sir, having coffee. Th-they all are.'

He nodded grimly. The floor seemed a long way down, the ceiling incredibly high and the distance through kitchen and butler's pantry unaccountably great, but he made his way out. He entered the hall and followed it determinedly, fighting against the trembling of his legs and trying to force air into his parched lungs. At the base of the elliptic stairs he reached out and clutched the newel for support and stood there weaving, fighting to regain his head.

The sound of voices came to him, and

after a moment he could sort them out. Lyman Ashton, Henrietta, Wick, Cissie Folwell. They were talking about Arthur Brokaw. Lambie Pie, apparently, had decided to go home to mother.

And then he heard Bill Donath's voice say, 'By the way, Lyman, I checked on your policies and you're covered on that damage to the glass doors. You'd better go over your stuff again and if anything was stolen let me have an inventory of it.'

'Nothing was stolen,' Ashton's voice denied quickly. 'Believe me, the motive wasn't robbery — '

He entered the library, and it was Henrietta who saw him first. Her face went chalky white and she whispered, '*Chris!*'

The others turned to look at him then, and quite suddenly his legs stopped trembling and he could breathe.

10

Their first shock changed swiftly to embarrassment.

Bill Donath apparently had not been with them at lunch. He was wearing his topcoat and carrying his hat. He started to say something about leaving and then his voice died away and he remained where he was. Cissie Folwell glared at him but did not speak, and Ashton's homely face, deeply red, was, after the first glance, averted.

Only Wick seemed to be in command of himself.

'Well, Christopher,' Wick said in a tired voice, 'I see you've finally managed to break in here. Naturally it would not have occurred to you that you could have entered legally and thus saved considerable embarrassment for all concerned. I suppose you're ready to raise hell.'

Christopher's eyes appraised him briefly and then sought Henrietta's white face. 'I've come to tell you a story,' he responded in a voice that was surprisingly gentle.

'I for one don't want to hear it,' Cissie announced harshly. 'I guess it isn't enough to build walls and hire guards. I suppose I'll have to call the police!'

'Do that, Mrs. Folwell,' An edge of steel crept into Christopher's voice. 'They'll be here shortly anyway. I believe your butler has already called them. But if you must do something, you might summon a physician for your 'guard' as you call him. He's almost as badly off as I was after my last visit here.'

Red-faced, Cissie subsided.

Henrietta glanced up at him. Her fine dark eyes held pleading. 'Please, Chris. This isn't the right way. You shouldn't have come here. You have no right to do this to me.'

'No. Of course I haven't the right. Whatever rights I might have had I've thrown away.' His voice became harsh as he turned to face Lyman Ashton. 'But there's one thing you've got to know and you might as well hear it from me. Our friend Lyman has a way with him. He gets what he wants, and his methods are simply out of this world. About nine months ago he wanted a house, and he got it by the simple expedient of scaring a poor woman half out of her wits. Bill, you were the agent for Five-Forty-Six Ridge Road; you'll remember Mrs. Holmes and the mouse she found on her pillow. You couldn't pay her to stay in the house after that, so Lyman obligingly took it off your hands.'

Bill Donath sat straighter. Colour came into his pinched cheeks. 'But Chris,' he objected, 'the same thing happened to Lyman, last night. There was another mouse. I saw it. I told him to go to the police.'

'Convenient, wasn't it? Didn't it strike you as rather odd that after Mrs. Holmes moved out there were no more mice until now? Don't you think it strange that all the other mice were planted with the utmost secrecy, while this last one was accompanied by a smashed door and a ransacked house?'

Bill Donath's eyes crystallized sharply.

Turning, he looked directly at Ashton. 'Well, what about it?' he asked coldly.

The writer laughed, a harsh cackle which he seemed unable to control. 'Preposterous — absurd — ' he cried through laughter.

They stopped looking at Christopher. They turned full on Ashton, and a kind of dawning horror was in their eyes.

'The last of the mice,' Christopher continued quietly, 'he inflicted on himself in a desperate attempt to divert suspicion. He knew his house had been ransacked and he guessed his secret had been discovered. But let's go back to the first mouse. It was a neat trick, so neat it was worth filing for reference. Having got the house he wanted he began to assemble the friends he wanted. He went at it through Bill Donath, the agent who had sold him the house. He was intelligent, witty, well-travelled, obliging and smooth. Bill liked him, and so he was introduced.'

Outside a car crunched on gravel, but if they heard it they made no sign. They were intent upon his words, but their eyes were weighing Ashton. They were judging him as only people of their kind can judge another of their kind. The intensity was merciless, and under it Ashton began to wilt.

'Unfortunately for him, fate did not permit his debut to be entirely unblemished. It was a grand party, given in the Donaths' best tradition, but there was one guest who should not have been present. The guest was a beautiful young woman named Ruth Cassell. Despite the fact that they both passed off the shock of their meeting and thereafter chose to ignore each other, it was ruinous for Ashton. He had been in love with her, had even offered her marriage, but she had retaliated with the most wounding insult a young girl can give an old man. She had told him to stop annoying her.'

Ashton winced, and for a moment Christopher felt almost sorry for him. But he plunged on. 'Ashton was deeply annoyed by her reappearance, but his annoyance turned to relief when he learned that she lived in the city and that her visit to Chelmere was a mere chance. He rose masterfully above his annoyance and became quite the life of the party, acting as master of ceremonies and assisting his host to introduce a new gadget, a recording machine. A little later on, about eight months later, that recorder was to furnish him with the means of making his neat little mouse trick complete.'

Ashton found his voice then. He started up. 'It's a lie,' he cried hoarsely. 'He's lying, I tell you! Don't listen to him! He's trying to save his own neck!'

It was Wick who pushed him down, 'I think we'll listen, Ashton,' Wick said coldly.

'Thank you, Wick. The rest is comparatively simple. Eight months after the chance meeting he discovered that Ruth Cassell had taken a cottage in Chelmere. He could see that cottage from his terrace; he could, on occasion, see her. Her presence soured his digestion and ruined his sleep. He could not imagine why she had come to Chelmere so he hired an unscrupulous detective named Malloy to dog her footsteps, and — '
Christopher faced Henrietta squarely

— 'through Malloy he learned that Ruth and I had been involved in an affair. When he learned this, in addition to wanting to get rid of her, he wanted to make her suffer. He knew how the business of the mice had affected poor Mrs. Holmes; he added to it the transcribed cry of a cat and the rest is newspaper history. He did his work well. He fooled me. He came to my home as a guest and during the evening found opportunity to visit my room and plant one of his detestable mice under my pillow. That was the master stroke. He was jealous and vindictive because, in his twisted mind, I had succeeded where he had failed. He wasn't content with driving Ruth Cassell from Chelmere: he wanted to hurt her, and me, as much as she had hurt him — '

Christopher clenched his hands. 'You rotten scum! You couldn't have known that Teena would find the dead mouse; you couldn't have foreseen how I would, because of your damnable cat business of the telephone, frighten her so that she will never again look at me with the same trust and devotion in her eyes — '

Someone grabbed his arms from behind and held him tightly. He struggled little; he was spent, shaking and ill.

★   ★   ★

He was back in Dickerson's office, seated in the same straight-backed chair. He was slumped down, gazing at a point between desk and floor but seeing nothing.

Dickerson came in through the corridor door, looked at him and shook his head. There were papers in the lieutenant's hands and he put them down. He wet his moustache with his lower lip, and shook his head again.

'I am indebted to you, Mr. Elliot,' Dickerson said in a sighing voice, 'for clearing up a difficult phase of this case for me, although I feel that if you had remained out of it we'd have got there just the same.'

'A phase?' Christopher brought his head up slowly. 'I don't believe I understand you.'

'The cat and mouse business was only

a phase. I do not deny it was an important phase; we needed the full solution of it to throw proper light on the murder of Ruth Cassell, but it was still only a phase.'

'Are you implying that Ashton didn't kill her?'

'You killed her, Mr. Elliot.'

The colour drained from Christopher's face. 'I?'

'Yes, Mr. Elliot.' Dickerson regarded him soberly. 'Were you a different sort of person, I might believe it possible that, considering the strain you were under, either you do not realize or you have forgotten. But I have no intention of outlining a defence for you. A man of your ego is apt to feel that murder is sometimes justifiable.'

Christopher relaxed. He grinned. 'So, you've finally got around to coming out with it.'

'I never speak until I am sure,' Dickerson replied soberly. 'Your basic reason for killing her was that she was destroying your ego. You'd had an affair with her. You had dismissed and dispatched her, but you could not drive her out. She was in you, imbedded so deep you had to cut her away by the surest means you knew.'

Christopher laughed. 'Really, Lieutenant. This is utterly absurd! Do you know what you're saying?'

'The event that changed you from a potential to an actual killer was Ashton's last bumbling attempt to get even with you and the woman he hated. After you'd heard his sound effects and when you saw the mouse in your daughter's hands, Ruth Cassell and her troubles and fears were forcibly projected into your home. In that moment it was not your small daughter, but Ruth Cassell who stood before you. I do not claim to be a psychologist, Mr. Elliot, but I believe you can be thankful for your wife's intervention at that point.'

Christopher stared in unspeaking amazement.

'You passed that crisis through no fault of your own, but you had to destroy Ruth Cassell. You did, finally, destroy her and it should have ended there, but somehow it didn't. After she was dead you received the third mouse and then you began to run in blind, crazy circles, trying to discover just where you'd gone wrong, doubling back on your tracks, trying to figure it out; there shouldn't have been a third mouse. Her death should have ended it, but it hadn't.'

The grin on Christopher's face had become a ghastly thing. 'How the devil did you know there was a third mouse? I never told you or anyone else.'

'I knew,' Dickerson answered quietly, 'because I sent it to you myself.'

★ ★ ★

Dickerson stepped to the exact centre of the worn green carpet, stiffened to attention and said, 'I believe you sent for me, sir.'

The commissioner looked up from a conglomeration of reports. Balling a fist that was as huge and hairy as a coconut he banged his desk and bellowed, 'Dickerson, have you lost your mind? Putting this Elliot in the tank? Charging him with murder? D'you know what he and Ed Kaufman will do to us?'

'They won't do anything to us, sir.'

'Hah! Don't you wish they won't! The Grand Jury will never indict him in a million years!'

'I beg your pardon, sir. The Grand Jury has indicted him. I've just returned from there.'

The commissioner's jaw dropped and his small round eyes opened wide. 'He — ' The commissioner covered his mouth with a hairy hand and scraped square fingers across his massive chin. 'Sit down, Dickerson,' he said in a choked voice.

Dickerson pulled up a chair and sat on the edge of it. 'We've got him so many ways, sir, it isn't even funny. To start, he told us he hadn't seen her since he put her on the bus in Chelmere Sunday night. But at the morgue he identified her from clothing she'd bought here in the city on Monday, the following day. I was with him when he identified her, and not once did he look beyond the clothing. He couldn't bring himself to look at her face. That was what started me on him.'

'But his alibi!' the commissioner groaned. 'You said yourself — all those people — that man Feeley — '

'It was too pat, sir. It looked from the outset as if he'd rigged it. At first we proceeded, because of the time element, on the assumption that he bought coffee and sandwiches *after* he killed her; there seemed to be a lapse of about ten minutes in there. And we couldn't figure just how he'd disposed of the pistol. But he had visited the Busy Bee *before* he went to the alley; he was carrying the bag of food when he met her. When she came toward him he spoke to her. Then he kissed her. And then he shot her.'

'*What?*' The commissioner looked as if he might be losing his mind. 'How in Hobb's Hollow are you going to prove it? Proof, Dickerson! That's all that counts!'

'We have it, sir. After he shot her he put down the paper bag, removed a pair of gloves he was wearing, dropped gloves and pistol into the bag, picked it up again and returned with it to his office. He was as cool as they come. He gave the janitor, Miggs, a carton of coffee and a sandwich from the bag which held, in addition to more coffee and sandwiches, the pistol and the gloves. With step number one in his alibi established, he found step number two just a bit ahead of schedule. Feeley called him fifteen minutes early. But Feeley could have made it still ten minutes earlier, because Elliot's timing was perfect. Step number three was to write the note, enclose fifteen dollars and give the envelope to Miggs. From there he went straight to the railway station where he ditched the paper bag in a parcel locker. He was smart enough not to lock it, or we'd've had him three days ago.'

The commissioner began to look as if he might survive after all. 'You have the bag and the pistol?'

'And the gloves.'

'All right, Dickerson. You say he kissed her. Prove it. You say he shot her. Prove it. You say the bag, gloves and pistol were his. Prove that too.'

'First, the bag. Schultz traced it to the Busy Bee. Even better than that, Pfeifer's microscope turned up scraps of bread and pressed ham of which the sandwiches were made. We may have trouble establishing the gloves as his, but on the inside right palm there is a line of blood corresponding exactly to the cut in his right hand; the force of the pistol's recoil opened the cut from top to bottom. And on the bottom of the paper bag the microscope turned up not only dust peculiar to the alley but also graphite and fragmented rubber eraser from the desk in Elliot's office.'

The commissioner died hard. 'The kiss,' he said. Dickerson nodded soberly. 'I wish we didn't have to use that, sir. He was really fond of her. We know he kissed her because of his habit, when excited, of wetting the end of a pencil with his lips. There was graphite on her lips, and Pfeifer said that while the quantity was insufficient for a detailed analysis, in his opinion the only possible source was a Hardmuth Koh-i-noor pencil, grade Two-B. Elliot has any quantity of them on his desk, and even had one in his pocket when we searched him yesterday. There was graphite from a pencil on her lips, but there was no pencil in her handbag and none in her room. She wrote a beautiful hand sir, and she never used anything but a fountain pen.'

We do hope that you have enjoyed reading this large print book.

Did you know that all of our titles are available for purchase?

We publish a wide range of high quality large print books including:
Romances, Mysteries, Classics General Fiction Non Fiction and Westerns

Special interest titles available in large print are:
The Little Oxford Dictionary Music Book, Song Book Hymn Book, Service Book

Also available from us courtesy of Oxford University Press:
Young Readers' Dictionary (large print edition) Young Readers' Thesaurus (large print edition)

For further information or a free brochure, please contact us at:
Ulverscroft Large Print Books Ltd., The Green, Bradgate Road, Anstey, Leicester, LE7 7FU, England. Tel: (00 44) 0116 236 4325 **Fax:** (00 44) 0116 234 0205